I. The P

There was much mirth in the House of Commons the day the legalisation of cannabis was discussed. The house giggled, the house snorted, the house wriggled in glee as the idea of 'making it legal, man' was mooted. Those that were able to keep straight faces delivered off-hand arguments about the need to abandon the war on drugs and adopt a less alienating position. Those that required no help in keeping a straight face argued forcefully for retaining the status quo and warned in dark tones of the imminent breakdown of society. In the end it came down to a free vote, the whips did not act because they were given no instructions, and each MP was left free to cast their own vote, which was mainly dependent on what their own personal experience of cannabis was. The vote was passed.

Decriminalisation, reclassification, authorisation and the licensing of a whole new industry, the civil service rubbed its' collective hands in eager anticipation of the administrative opportunities. Setting up the new agency alone would mean six hundred and fifty new jobs and at the very minimum a twenty-two point eight million pound budget. Even prior to the vote contending government departments had been vying for the right to oversee the new legislative body. The health, business and culture departments all claimed a crucial need in having a say in the policies, conduct and actions of the licensing authority. So the stage was set, the politicians had decided yes to a major change, the legislative body began drawing up systems, regulations and penalties, and the public at large braced itself for the shock of finally being granted what it was it apparently wanted.

Jim was working in a jeweller's. Jim liked working with jewels, but it didn't pay well, and there was no chance of him moving up in the business, the same family had owned it for three hundred years, and the next generation were preparing themselves to take over, and as Jim joshed with himself there was no option of marrying into the business either, the next generation were very male and very straight. So Jim enjoyed away his days working in the shop preparing and selling gems for girls with a glint in their eye. He often dreamt of one day putting a glint in a girl's eye himself, but Jim knew that under his current circumstances were he to invite any girl home to his flat, the flat he shared with his brother, his divorced brother who had his thirteen year old daughter over to stay every other weekend, plus each time she had a row with her mother, Jim knew if he ever invited a girl back to his present home he wouldn't even initiate the hint of a glint.

In due course the cabinet heard submissions from the departments of health, business and culture as to why it was they who should be the body to oversee the newly named Cannabis Licensing Authority, the CLA. Every government department that submitted a tender made the same proposal, that it should be an independent agency, very much a non-governmental organisation, that should have absolute responsibility for anything and everything that might go wrong with legalising a formerly prohibited substance. In addition every government department agreed most vigorously that it was vital for this independent agency to be irrevocably accountable and answerable to a government department, headed by a lawfully elected politician, and that that department should have absolute responsibility for any and all perceived and actual benefits that might stem from the act of legalisation. The department of health fielded the argument that as they would no doubt be the recipient of many of those who experienced the benefits of legalisation it should be health that adopts the position of overseer. Business and Trade insisted that as the whole reason for legalisation was to raise tax revenues it should automatically be they who must be allowed to regulate the expected windfall generated by the CLA. Culture, Media and Sport pitched that it obviously fell under their remit. People often take cannabis to enhance their enjoyment of whatever culture they choose. The whole process of legalisation had frequently been described as a culture change, clearly this was a cultural issue.

Cabinet was supplied with a lengthy and detailed submission from each government department, they discussed it for four and a half minutes and decided it should go to health. The cabinet secretary insisted that as the treasury was funding the setting up of the CLA it must also have a seat alongside health on the over-seeing regulatory committee, to which the cabinet agreed and the system was put in place. Civil servants seconded from the health department and the treasury clubbed together and then they in turn employed further civil servants, who all came together to form the core of the CLA.

Once established the CLA then became the body to which all parties who wished to sell cannabis legally should apply. The plan being that when a serious application was received they would, for a significant fee, undertake an examination of the premises from which the business would be run, the security arrangements in place, the character of the person applying for a licence, and if following that assessment a licence was granted, the continued monitoring and evaluating of how and in what manner that business was conducted. The first dilemma was where to site the agency. Its' location would inevitably bring some notoriety, and possibly be the centre of some form of future campaigns, a disused police station in south west London was found to possess the appropriate qualities, though what had been good enough for police officers was certainly not of standard for civil servants so twenty-six builders, seven carpenters, and an unquantifiable number of interior designers went to work for three weeks with the first two million of the budget to ensure that a hundred and fifty permanent civil servants, and a discrete number of privately-contracted consultants, would have a pleasant environment to work in for the coming few years.

Jim was striving for success. He knew where he was, he was at level zero. Basic job, seriously basic home, good internet feed. He enjoyed jewels, but as he often joked to himself, he knew jewels would never bring him riches. He did not want that joke to become the basis of his life. Jim read the newspapers, he had laughed heartily when he first read about the setting up of the CLA. 'Whoever runs the first legal dope shop is going to make a mint,' he thought. That thought stayed with Jim. It stayed with him throughout his working week, throughout his tending and retailing of his precious treasures. It lurked at the back of his mind during his TV watching of a weekday night, he joked about it with his one remaining single mate in the pub on a Friday evening. Jim still had the thought in the back of his mind on Sunday afternoon when he met a man in the park at the bench by the kiddies' playground. Jim had been meeting the same man most Sundays for getting on fifteen years now. The man would chat for a while, as was his want, and in recent years often while attending to his daughter who had a penchant for hanging upside down underneath the climbing frame. When the man was comfortable money would pass from Jim to him, forty pounds, sixty pounds, eighty or more if Jim was feeling flush, and a corresponding number of small plastic bags containing a bright green herb would pass gracefully back to a grateful Jim. Jim frequently wondered if his Sunday afternoon meetings might ever so slightly be under-mining his own desire to achieve success. However the thought that he could not shift, the thought of guaranteed riches for the first legal marijuana retailer, appeared to Jim to be the perfect antidote to this fear. So on this particular Sunday afternoon as he met the man on the bench, and as the man began his chat, in a swift but appropriate moment, Jim gave voice to his thought.

"You know they're setting up this thing now called the CLA, the cannabis licensing authority, they're going to licence the legal selling of dope. Whoever sets up the first shop is going to make a million !"

"And you think you're the man ?"

Jim did pause for a moment, but he knew the answer was yes, so he said it.

"Yes."

"Ahh so you do think you're the man."

"I think I am the man that could apply to the CLA and have them say yes. I've never been arrested, always paid my taxes. And I think, no I know, that I am the man that having got that licence could run that shop and make a very healthy profit indeed, the first and only legal source of marijuana in town, your market is wide-spread and guaranteed ! The difficulty would be keeping up with demand."

"I could."

"I'm sure you could but what I lack is the start-up costs, the premises, the cost of converting them, the application fee.."

"I could cover that."

Jim looked at the man, the man had a straight face.

"It's like you say, the first legal and institutionally approved herb shop, man that will be a place to be. Now me, I might have difficulty getting a licence for such a thing, but you, that's a distinct possibility, and I'm happy to fund that."

"Could you fund that ?"

"You're not my only customer."

"But you barely know me, I don't think I even know your name."

"Boy I have sold you dope every week for the past fifteen years, I know your soul. I trust you. I'll supply, you distribute, all completely legal."

Jim looked at the man, the man looked back at Jim, the man grinned, Jim grinned. Jim nodded. Then the man did something he had never done before, as he leant forward and patted Jim on his shoulder while subtly passing him two plastic packets with his lower hand, he whispered quietly into Jim's ear, "keep your cash, this one's on me."

The man grinned once more, stood up, twirled, said, "see you next week, sharpish." And with his palm held in the air as a parting gesture the man was gone.

Jim remained seated. He looked about him, no-one was watching, he opened his clenched hands and inspected the plastic bags, they were to his liking, he reclenched his hand. Jim grinned. Jim could not stop grinning, he found himself grinning a very large grin indeed. Now he felt truly self-conscious. Sitting on his own on the park bench by the playground was bad enough, but sitting there and being unable to stop smiling really wasn't right. Jim took a walk across the park, his grin remained in place.

For the first time in many a long year Jim did not hurry home after making his Sunday afternoon purchase. He remained walking in the park conducting a most coherent train of thought. 'This could actually happen.. Yes ! Right calm down and think what you can do to make it really happen. Well in reality the situation remains exactly the same as it ever was, basic job, basic home, good internet feed, right, that's it, play to your strengths, good internet, a CLA application is possible and affordable using the man's money and contacts, so the next question is how to hide the source of the money, well come to think of it the man probably has some experience of that already, the only thing to do is simply wait until next Sunday to ask him more questions, simply wait.' Jim held onto this thought, he reassuringly squeezed the two plastic bags in his pocket, turned and headed for home.

Jim greeted Monday morning more enthusiastically than he ever had before, he dashed to the wardrobe to get his clothes, he sung his request for usage of the bathroom when discovering his niece was in occupation. He laid out the breakfast items on the kitchen table, an act that never had been done in this particular home before. When his brother raised a quizzical eyebrow he simply replied, "well why not do things differently once in a while ?" The eyebrow lowered, his niece relinquished her occupancy of the bathroom, bundled into the kitchen and stopped in stunned silence at the sight of a neatly laid kitchen table. "What the..." Three eyebrows raised in preventative anticipation, two from Jim's brother, one from Jim. The girl, acknowledging the eyebrows, continued, "what an amazing thing, there's not bad news is there ?" "No," replied Jim, "I just thought it'd be nice to do things differently for a change, please enjoy." And with that Jim slipped into the bathroom and enjoyed a thoroughly vigorous shower and shave.

Monday morning at work was rarely a busy time in the jeweller's. Hence Jim spent a quiet morning taking pride in his work place. He dusted the velvet display cases, he sucked the dirt from the fluorescent bulbs, he gave the windows a good wipe and as is most important in a jeweller's, he applied oil to all the hinges and castors, drawers and cupboards. In a jeweller's the display cases should slide open rather than groan. Later on in the morning one of the shop owners popped in, not the head of the family but a favoured uncle, he noted the care that had been taken in the presentation of the shop.

"Thinking of leaving us James ?" Muttered the uncle.

Jim stood in stunned silence, he could think of no lies that the uncle would believe, and the truth would simply be inappropriate, he opted for a half-truth, "I have been made an offer."

“A good offer ?”

“An uncertain offer.”

“When will you know more ?”

“After the weekend.”

“Then we’ll speak next week.” The uncle surveyed the shop, “nice job.” He then jingled the keys to the underground safe room and disappeared down the cellar steps.

Jim took his lunch hour at noon. As he had previously planned he visited the library to make use of their net access. Odd he thought to himself that having identified his only real strength as decent connectivity that his first action was to specifically avoid using it, but he felt no need to give himself away on the first day. He contemplated trying to conceal his identity from the cameras in the library, though his business-like train of thought pointed out that if he was to be the acceptable face of this operation he may as well get used to showing his face. So he took his seat on the rickety plastic chair, stuck his chin out purposefully towards the screen and typed CLA into the search engine.

The twenty-six builders and seven carpenters had been joined by four plasterers, six tilers and a dozen carpet fitters. The number of interior designers still remained uncertain. Their three weeks of work had become four, not that the labourers hadn’t finished on time, but having inspected the building the emerging nucleus of CLA officials requested further improvements to the revamped police station. The cell area rather than simply being sealed off was converted into a series of saunas, steam rooms and showers. Frosted glass dividers replaced the steel doors. The CCTV was removed and where the custody desk once stood now became a bar and dining area. The over-run to the budget would be explained to the spending review committee, due to be convened within between six and eighteen months following the completion of the project, as a very necessary cost to help maintain the health and welfare of the CLA staff, as no doubt they will have faced an extremely stressful time managing the CLA and the spending review committee would simply have to accept that it was essentially a saving to have installed stress reduction measures well in advance of the anticipated stress.

The thirty staff who had formed the core of the CLA took occupancy of the building and went to work. They all met, made each other tea, discussed the new building, established the social class of one another, and then sat down and decided what they should do. Clearly they had the perfect environment for applicants to come and present their case, the former interview rooms despite being given a lick of paint still managed to retain a drab and intimidating nature. The new CLA core staff agreed that the first topic on their agenda must be the employing of more staff. Creating a CLA website was topic number two. It was quickly decided there would be no logo, there didn't feel the need to provide the satirists which such obvious ammunition. It was agreed that the first purpose of the website would be to record the details of those people visiting the website. Its' second purpose would be to provide access to an overly long and off-putting form, peppered with red warnings highlighting the need for checkability and accountability for all entries on the form and threatening severe fines for any inaccuracies regardless of the success of the application. The actual checks on the applicants would be undertaken by an internet search, interview and site visit. Establishing the fee they would charge provoked intense debate. The arguments ranged from the point of view that the fee should be fairly expensive in order to deter time wasters and spurious applications to the argument that the fee should be prohibitively expensive as essentially selling drugs, even if state authorised, should actually be deterred. In the end the figure of twenty-five thousand pounds was chosen with a yearly fee of fifteen thousand pounds per annum thereafter. The CLAians then began to work out the penalties and regulations.

Jim perused the website. He did not begin the application. He was deterred by dire warnings of heavy fines for any omissions or inaccuracies. He was able to study and note the criteria expected of an applicant. 1) The CLA authorised retailer should have no previous criminal convictions and should not have been declared bankrupt or be in receipt of any court judgements against them. 2) The CLA authorised retailer should be able to provide premises that are pejorative to the safe and secure distribution of narcotic products. 3) The retailer shall ensure that the distribution of narcotic products is carried out with full regard for the welfare of the consumer. There were twenty-two points in all, Jim noted them down word for word rather than print out the list, he felt he took in information better that way. He took the piece of paper, folded it, and placed it inside his jacket pocket. Confident he had learned what he wanted to learn he rose from his seat, it was twelve fifty-five and work was a four minute walk away, his eye caught the security camera covering the area around the computers, Jim winked and exited the library.

Monday afternoon passed as it usually did in the jewel shop. Around three o'clock a lightly dressed blonde dragged a man of Arabic appearance into the store, she giggled and stroked for eight minutes, he paid out seventy thousand pounds. An elderly couple came in after that, she smiled hopefully, he winced and held his chest, they left quietly. Five o'clock arrived and Jim gently shut the shop door, he swiftly checked the locks on all windows, doors and display cases, then called hesitantly down the cellar stairs, "Sir I'm shutting up the shop now." "Right you are James," came the muffled reply.

Jim walked home. It was a choice. The bus would have taken about twenty-five minutes, a walk an hour and a quarter. In the bus he would have felt carried, by walking he felt in control, and it was time for thought undisturbed by another passenger's foibles.

Jim quickly escaped the commercial city streets which surrounded the jewellery store, taking first a canal path before tying a luminous bandolier around his chest and walking along a cycle path out of the heart of the city. His mind began ticking down the CLA conditions. Number one, no convictions, bankruptcies or court judgements, tick, it was not all men in their thirties who could state that without fear of contradiction Jim commended to himself. Number two, premises, time to start hunting he thought. Jim could picture the necessary security arrangements, the same as they had in the jeweller's, a locked door, possibly even two in an air-lock arrangement, and a proven and maintained link to security operatives and the police. Also a plan would need to be in place should anyone successfully con their way inside, Jim felt confident that with his experience he could satisfactorily tick this box. Condition three, the welfare of the consumer, now this was a new one on Jim, very few people had ever expressed concern for the welfare of people buying jewellery. Jim imagined his dope shop was now open, with a long line of eager customers, and the lead customer was unable to speak. That customer would have to be swiftly moved on thought Jim, maybe thought Jim he could follow that up with providing them with some literature on the dangers of drugs. Maybe it would become necessary to develop a proven and maintained link to the local accident and emergency department as well considered Jim. It was definitely a subject he would have to contemplate and develop a clear and coherent policy on, and he mentally placed half a tick against box number three.

On his Tuesday night walk home Jim composed the questions he would have to ask the man. First and foremost was what would Jim declare as the source of the money. Jim wondered if he would be expected to go down the classic a relative remembered me in their will route. He reckoned given a little time with photoshop he could produce the life story of a much loved, now dearly departed half-sister. The lies began to flow, his mother's first marriage had been more successful, and all the money had gone to Lizzie, but alas in her late forties she'd developed cancer and after a brief but valiant fight.. He felt he could carry off the story but there just wouldn't be the paperwork to back it up. He returned to the truth for a moment. The money to set up the drug dealing shop was coming from a drug dealer. As practical a situation as it was it still didn't sound socially defendable or economically reliable. He began to mentally fill in the details of Elizabeth's life.

On Wednesday's commute Jim was happy to take the bus. He had reached what he felt was a less crucial subject on his mental check list, a name for the business and possibly an accompanying logo. Jim didn't really feel the need for anything eye-catching, something subtle and quite possibly a picture of 'the leaf' worked into the image. He was looking for inspiration so he was happy to let the other passengers, the public, his future customers influence him. When he was confident no-one had their eye on him Jim glanced over his fellow travellers, all bar two were looking at or listening to their phones, of the other two one was sleeping, the other appeared to be thinking. He left those two to their thoughts and dreams and appraised the persons perusing their phones. A young man with a keen look in his eye was making repeated darting movements towards a white and blue logo on his phone, right thought Jim, a white and blue logo it is. His mind conjured a picture of a white planet encircled by a blue sash, and on that sash was written the word legal followed by the universally acknowledged image of a cannabis leaf. His business would do exactly what it said on the logo, "right" muttered Jim to himself, that's the name sorted, so that's tick tick tick. Another passenger looked up from their phone in his general direction, Jim gently closed his eyes, then kept them screwed shut for the rest of the journey.

For Thursday's trip home Jim walked the bus route. He had toyed with the idea of taking the bus then jumping off early and walking the last few kilometres, but as there hadn't been a bus when he arrived at the first stop he simply started to walk. His first task of any Thursday evening, contact single mate Rob to see if he was around for Friday night. Jim sent his message off, Rob had confirmed his availability within five minutes. 'Should I discuss the plan ?' with Rob thought Jim. His brain replied with a yes. The only reason to not tell his friend his plans was if he wasn't sure they were going to work out, and Jim knew he was going to do this, he'd been researching, planning, preparing all week and was quite aware that the next crucial meeting was with the man on Sunday, telling Rob his plans would not effect that so there was no reason not to tell him, so right thought Jim, this Friday night I really do have a story to tell my mate.

Clink.

"So how's your week been?"

Jim smiled in response to the question.

"So is that good, bad, weird ?"

"Good ! Definitely good. I'm putting a plan together, going for it, going for the upgrade mate."

"Great. Good on yer, can you talk about it, or is it a secret plan.."

"Yes and no. Really. Okay are you ready for this, because this is really happening, and yes you should know about this, so, you ready ?.."

"I'm ready, I'm ready."

"The CLA."

"You're going to apply for a job with the cannabis licensing authority.."

"For a licence."

"You're going to run a dope shop..."

"I'm going to run a dope shop. I run the jeweller's. I shmoke a dee dope. I run the dope shop."

Clink.

Saturday morning rolled around and Jim didn't see the need to leave his bed. He had his plan, he had rehearsed his questions, he was focused on Sunday's meeting, this was now just waiting time. Jim contemplated doing some exercise. Two o'clock Saturday afternoon rolled around, Jim's brother knocked on the door, he spoke a muffled "yow", Jim too replied, "yow", the muffled voice continued, "taking kiddo down the cinema, it's on me if you wanna join us." "What you watching ?" "What she wants if you're not there, what we want if you are." "I'm there."

The film was followed by food, then Jim, brother Steve and his daughter Imogen were back in the flat by ten o'clock, she immediately swept into the guest room swearing she would post a bad review of their movie choice, the brothers took a beer each and sunk into their usual seats.

"So," began Steve, "something's up."

"You think something's wrong ? " Eyebrowed Jim.

"No. It's more like something's right. You just seem more.. attentive."

"Yes well I am going to go for it brother, go for the upgrade, biggish meeting tomorrow, we'll see how it goes from there."

"And when you say 'going for the upgrade' what exactly do you mean ? "

"Applying to run my own shop, not just be the shop assistant anymore."

"Good on you brother, if I can help in anyway, let me know."

"Cheers."

Sunday morning arrived, now Jim rolled over and over. He tried to consider every aspect of his afternoon meeting, his demeanour, his tone, the order and importance of his questions, Jim tried to silence his brain just so he could practice listening. His brain wouldn't silence, 'right' thought Jim, exercise it is, 'if I stay here I'll go mad, I just have to move around.' Jim briefly contemplated having a smoke but he knew the necessity to have a clear mind over rid all else. He found socks and trainers and what looked like a pair of shorts, grabbed a t-shirt and his headphones, and then Jim went for a genuine jog around the park. He soon found himself circling the playground area, checking for anything unusual or new in the vicinity, but quickly realised he hadn't actually looked around the park before so was really in no position to judge. He counted two litter bins, three dog bins, nineteen trees and eight street lights covering the all-weather pathway, no CCTV that he could spot. Jim's ankles hurt and his breath felt wheezy but his mind was occupied.

Jim arrived home at midday, sweaty and panting, the bathroom was occupied. "I'll just be a minute !" Rang out Imogen's sing-song voice over the sound of her music, shower and phone conversation that were all audible through the bathroom door. Jim winced, fortunately Steve was on hand to see the wince and stepped up, his stage whisper was audible throughout the flat, "Imogen if you vacate the bathroom in the next sixty seconds it's yours from one o'clock for the rest of the day." "Oh Dad I'll just be like, ten minutes." "Imogen.. twenty pounds and a lift to and picking-up from a venue of your choice tonight, no questions asked, if you vacate in.." The door flew open, Imogen smiled, "Thank you," uttered Steve, and Jim dove into the shower.

He was on the park bench fifteen minutes before their usual time. And seeing as their usual time was anywhere from quarter to-ish until quarter past-ish this was remarkably early. Jim stared straight ahead, his mind was clear. He maintained his calm, he maintained his direct point of view, until he felt the presence of the man taking the seat beside him.

"So you are up for it."

"I am up for it."

"Good. What do you know ? "

"The cost of a CLA application is twenty-five thousand pounds. The annual fee is fifteen thousand pounds. They want to know about the security arrangements, the character of the retailer, the plans in place for customer care, I can provide positive answers to all of these."

"Excellent. What do they want to know about the gear and where it comes from ?" "They don't ask that on the website. It must come up in the interview, I'll make the application and see what they ask. I don't think the law is actually being changed, it's just being amended to allow possession of dope by authorised licensees on authorised premises. So I don't know if that means we'll be expected to produce on site. Is that possible ?"

"Yes if you've got some damn big caves. I mean I want to go Amsterdam with this shit. A menu with a myriad of possibilities, we do need to know what we're allowed to do."

The man paused.

Jim waited.

"Retail premises, we have."

"Good."

The man paused again, Jim waited once more.

"Um, where ?"

"Well it has to be a London borough see, no way they'd allow this shit in the counties. Now at first no borough's gonna want you either, but once we're set up and established, they'll be battling it out to set up the sweet shop next door. But how to get that first foot in the door, I mean I reckon those posh North London places would lap this up, but the rents man, not a chance. Gotta go cheaper man, gotta go Croydon."

“Croydon.“

“I know a man who knows a man who already has a shop unit in South Croydon, it used to be a vape shop but then they discovered the truth about what them electric things do to your lungs, the unit’s available now.”

“I’d like to see it.”

“You can. It’s Croydon, they’re used to being robbed, there’s steel shutters that roll down, it looks the part.”

“Brilliant. The money ?”

“The money ?”

“What do I tell the CLA about where the money comes from ?”

“Why do they need to know ?”

“They don’t. But what if they ask ?”

“You took out a loan ?”

“They might want to see paperwork.”

“Mmm..”

“I had this thought, it could have been left to me by Elizabeth, err my deceased half-sister, my brother would back-up the story.”

“You work for a jeweller’s right ?”

“You know that..”

“I know that.”

“Okay.”

“Say it was loaned to you by your employer, they’re more likely to believe a wealthy jew is investing in the business that some fortuitously dead sister.”

Mmm. You know what, that works. Okay so when do we do the site visit, application, and sit down and work out the logistics of paying the fee ?”

“Your timetable my man.”

“I’ll have a conversation with my employer tomorrow, and I’ll contact you in the normal way tomorrow night.”

The man responded with a hand grab and fist bump.

"So do we have a name for our business ?"

"Legal followed by the leaf symbol."

"Mmm like it, until tomorrow.."

"Until tomorrow."

Jim attempted a fist bump but lost his nerve half way through, the man accommodated. The man departed and once more Jim was left alone with his smile, not the huge grin of the previous week, but a very definite half-smile. He cast a few thoughts towards the conversation he would be having at the jeweller's tomorrow, but realised he didn't even know who he'd be having the conversation with, though he already knew what his own tone and demeanour would be, but found himself stumbling over one of the questions that he really should ask ? Did he want the option of going back ? Should 'the plan' not lead to profit did he want the security of knowing he would be allowed back, or should he not want that, should he not even be contemplating such a thing ? Well clearly he was contemplating it so Jim considered the question, would he want to go back ? Jim looked up, he spied the man walking out of the park, a pair of excited teenagers were running away from him at top speed, they paused breathlessly behind a tree to furtively examine what they held in their hands. Looking back to the man Jim saw that he'd now met someone else by the park entrance, a man pushing a pram, the two were chatting amiably until the dad accidentally dropped his baby's coat on the ground, fortunately the man was on hand to carefully pick it up and return it to him. 'You know what,' Jim thought to himself, 'I don't think they'll be a need to return to the jeweller's.'

Monday. Jim arrived at work at eight forty-five, the alarm was off and he could hear voices from the cellar. The popular uncle was saying, “Indeed I will,” to someone who remained in the basement. The uncle then shuffled his way up the steps and greeted Jim with a smile, Jim smiled warmly in return.

“Well my boy did you have your meeting ?”

“I did, and it’s an opportunity I’d like to take.”

The uncle gazed at Jim, blinking intermittently behind his glasses. “Let me ask you this, what might you gain, what might you lose ?”

“Riches, possibly, but at the very least management of my own shop, management of my own destiny. What I might lose..” Jim turned his palms outward. “Well this, security, familiarity, stability.”

“Indeed, well one must try, one must try,” muttered the uncle, “are you staying in the gem business James ?”

“No I’ll be retailing a new product to the market.”

“Oh yes.”

“Yes Sir, I’m not so sure you’d approve, but I am very confident of the demand.”

“Oh well you’ve rather answered my inquiry there, Jim, mazel tov to you my boy.”

Jim looked quizzical.

“Oh well, Argentina, Austria, Bolivia, Chile, Costa Rica, Czech republic, Ecuador, Estonia, Germany, Luxembourg, Malta, Moldova, Portugal, South Africa, Uruguay, and over thirty American states, I was still surprised though, I thought it would take England another fifty years at least !”

Jim laughed. “So you think it’s a viable business?”

“My boy for ten years now I have seen you serve in this shop. From the gangsters to the millionaires and all those in between and I have never seen you bat an eye-lid. I am sure you are the man to provide England with its’ marijuana. Do please stay in touch Mr James Pemberton.”

“Thank you Sir.” Jim passed back the keys to the shop and they clenched one another’s hands as they did so. Jim smiled, shut his eyes, turned to face the shop doorway, re-opened his eye with his gaze fixed firmly through the doorway and exited the shop. He did not look back. Jim texted the man as he walked the bus route. ‘Plans brought forward from tonight to now, site visit ?’ Jim had walked a further two kilometres before receiving a reply. ‘Possible, can you make it to Croydon ?’ ‘I’ll take the tram can be at George Street in an hour’ Jim replied, his text was liked.

II. Croydon

The shop building looked hard. Clad in concrete, two stories of flats above, five retail units across the bottom, two were empty, one was a laundrette, the vape shop, and a take-away claiming to serve the best quality Chinese, Indian and Thai fare and Fish & Chips. The vape shop was in the centre, the five units shared a car park of eighteen spaces at the rear, protected by twisting metal grilles atop a brick wall, and a raiseable metal pole at the car park entrance. "We might have to improve that to a set of gates," suggested Jim to the man." "I'll get that costed up," he responded.

The inside of the shop was standard, two display islands, a counter half way back with a false wall behind it, behind that wall the rear of the shop, a toilet, store room and an exit out to the car park. There was no air-lock system to the door but a grille that rolled down covering the glass frontage of the shop.

"All product must be on the wall behind the counter. Pipes, papers and bongs on the display islands. There has to be a grill that comes down, or a reinforced door or something for the staff to get behind at the back of the counter area." Jim then thought for a moment. "I'd be more in favour of the grill, protect the stock as well as the staff. Or.. We could go full on bank style, bulletproof glass and talking through a sieve." The man listened to Jim's words, then positioned himself between the display islands at the front of the shop and walked up to the imaginary future counter and gazed upon the soon-to-be stock wall behind it. "Nah man," said the man, "I want it to be.. ..service with a smile !" The man himself smiled and the room became a little bit brighter. "But.." Continued the man, "..this is Croydon so I'll have two big fuckers stationed on the door at all times."

Jim nodded his approval. He took his place behind the counter and greeted an imaginary customer, "Well Sir, what will it be today ? We have skunk, sinsemilla, maui wauie. We have buba kush, hindu kush, purple haze, white widow, and of course, a little willie nelson."

"Oh my man !" Said the man, rubbing his hands in imaginary glee, "you know today I would like a blend of them all, and I want my spilff hand-rolled on a virgin's thigh !"

Jim rolled his eyes round the perimeter of the shop, "sorry, fresh out of virgin's round here." Jim grinned and slapped both his hands onto the counter breaking the spell. "Right I'm taking pictures of the premises." "Then" replied the man, "I'm hiding my pretty face away, meet you out back when you're done." "Before you disappear" retorted Jim swiftly, "what do I say about the premises ?" "The current shop manager is a personal ally and completely on-board, the lease is secured for the next eighteen months, and it's barely even a change of use with regards to the business activities, also do tell them that we will happily implement any security features they want us to install, capiche ?" "Capiche." "Meet you out back when you're done."

The man exited to the car park and Jim proceeded to take photos of the shop floor, of the back rooms, of the shop's entry and exit points, trying to cover every angle the CLA might question him on. Once he was satisfied he had all the pictures he might need he too left through the back of the shop. The man was sharing a smoke with the chef from the take-away. Jim approached hesitantly, the man waived him closer, the chef spoke to the man's shoes, "anytime yeah ?" "Anytime" the man responded warmly, and the chef nodded, pulled up his collar, and stumbled back in the direction of his kitchen.

“Walk with me back to the station if you would,” said the man.

“Gladly,“ responded Jim.

They walked.

“So you like the shop ?”

“I like the shop.”

“You ready for this ?”

“I’m ready for this.”

“Then we’ve talked.”

“Man, the money, what are the logistics of paying for this application.”

“We set up an account in the name of the shop, I put thirty k in it. I’d have it set up already only you can’t call an account legal leaf symbol, we need like a written name for the account.”

“I get it”

“So legal weed, legal dope, cannabis is us..”

“Somehow I don’t want to go down the route of dope or weed, our thing is a legal thing.”

“So it is Jim, Legal Jim’s.”

“Legal Jims ?”

“Legal Jims.” The man smiled his radiating smile. “You got ID ?” “Uh huh.” “Then let’s set up that account right now ‘Legal Jim’ and let’s get rolling !”

The staff members of the Cannabis Licencing Authority now numbered one hundred and two. There were administrative staff, interviewing staff, greeters, fact checkers, security officers, liaison officers, building maintenance staff, cleaners, and independent contractors contributing all manner of premium skills. Depending on which of the contracted accountants you believed either fifteen point four or eighteen point two million pounds had been spent so far, without as yet a licence being issued. The website had been open for four weeks, and had been viewed some seven hundred thousand times, but of the handful of applications actually received, several had failed the 'please complete in English requirement', none had provided details of how payment would be made, and in the odd case where an application had looked promising the CLA phoned the applicant back only for the applicant to deny that it was they who had applied. The expected cloud of social change predicted by the newspapers did not appear to be forming very rapidly. This didn't cause too much concern in the ranks of the CLA. It was not their role to promote drug use, as the secretary to the assistant communications director explained, only to regulate it. The media soon questioned why there was a need for a regulatory body without an industry and within weeks of it opening the newspapers began to demand sackings at the CLA.

On the Monday night of the morning he had left the jewellers Jim sat down and prepared to tackle the CLA website. Jim had his cup of tea to his right, his paperwork to his left, the photos on his mobile phone by the side of the keyboard, and the door to his room firmly shut, with a sausage dog draught excluder helping dampen outside sounds. He began. He supplied his name, his date of birth, his national insurance number, his employment history, his credit history, Jim gave permission for his medical history to be his accessed, for his image to be checked against all databases, he agreed to supply a DNA swab and birth certificate at a later date, and was asked to provide referees relating to his work and character. Jim ticked yes to all the boxes he thought he should tick yes to, and no to all the boxes he thought he should answer no to. Two hours later he leant back from the computer, ran his fingers through his hair, checked over the screen once more, nodded his approval of his answers and clicked apply. Only then did Jim skin up.

It was a good spliff. It was a most satisfying spliff. It was a 'I've done what I had to do and now I'm ree- lax... ...ing' spliff. Jim curled his toes, he stretched his calves, he stuck his arms straight out from his sides and vigorously wiggled his fingers, he made no attempt to hide the smile from his face. 'Yes', he thought, 'there may well be a storm coming, but I've battened down the hatches and my ship is prepared.' Jim drifted off to sleep that night and didn't wake till gone nine the following morning.

When he did wake he was coaxed into life by the gentle vibrating of his mobile phone, it was his voicemail calling, he accepted the call in a dreary state and placed the phone to his ear, an inhuman voice informed him he was called today at nine zero one and then played him the message, there was no sound, it went on for three minutes.

Jim left the phone off while he had his cereal and switched on the morning news, feeling suitably sated he sat down and switched on his computer at around ten o'clock, fourteen new messages. Four were from a Canadian pharmacy, two from Nigeria, three informed him of lottery wins and two were from girls wishing to meet him but without the funds to travel. The last three e-mails mattered. One was from the bank confirming his access to the Legal Jim bank account, and two were from the Cannabis Licencing Authority, one an automated e-mail (Jim assumed) sent in the early hours acknowledging his application, and a second sent that morning inviting him to get in touch in order to arrange an interview.

Jim stopped, got up from the computer and went to look in the bathroom mirror, to really look at the bathroom mirror. He assessed his unkempt hair, each blotch on his skin, his mis-shapen teeth, 'well' he thought to himself, 'it's a business application, not a beauty contest, be relaxed, be confident, have the answers.' He nodded to the mirror his affirmation he could do that, showered, shaved, put on a clean shirt, checked his smartened appearance in the mirror, and only then did Jim sit down to reply to the CLA.

He resisted the urge to click every box when offered interview times, selecting instead only afternoon slots, hoping his interviewers would be feeling well-fed and agreeable at that time. By eleven Jim had completed his reply and also texted the man the news he was at the interview stage. He received a smiley face in return.

He received a phone call in response to his e-mail.

"Good morning, this is the Cannabis Licensing Authority calling. Is this Mr James Pemberton ?"

"Yes it is."

"And have you recently completed an application to become an authorised cannabis retailer on the CLA website ?"

"Yes I have."

"And do you wish to proceed with that application ?

"Yes I do."

The phone line went quiet for a moment, Jim thought he heard a faint cheer in the background.

"Right then Sir, the next stage of the application is an interview. I see you have made yourself available for the afternoon slots, how would tomorrow afternoon at two suit you ?"

"That would suit me fine."

"Good, our address is on the website, please do bring all paperwork as requested in the application and we shall see you tomorrow."

Jim and the caller thanked each other and Jim swiftly closed the call careful not to let any of his background noises become audible. When he was confident his mobile had shut down the line and the call had finished beyond a shadow of doubt Jim placed the phone carefully on the flat surface in front of him, and then punched the air in screaming silent glee. 'Oh yes, oh YES, OH YES !' yelled his brain. Stage one was complete, stage two was under way, the next vital moment had become tomorrow afternoon, would he be sober, would he be prepared, would he be good, oh yes he knew he would. Would the CLA unconditionally grant his application ? That he could not control, but Jim knew he would put forward his case to the absolute best of ability, this was his shot, his aim would be true. Jim willed it to be twenty-four hours from now , he tried to force time forward one day to bring it to the point where he was standing in front of that address in South West London, papers in hand, ready to face the CLA inquisition feeling as he did right now.

Jim couldn't make it happen, it remained Tuesday. Practicality set in. He felt a conversation with the man would be in order, Jim texted him a smiling face with a raised eyebrow. The man texted back a face with two raised eyebrows. Jim texted back, 'can we have a conversation.' The man texted back, 'I do text or face-to-face.' Jim replied, 'It's okay, we're legal now.' There was a pause in the man's replies. After a few minutes came the text, 'Okay I'll call you.' Jim received a call from an unknown number a few moments later.

"Man ?"

"Tis me."

"Okay so the interview is set for tomorrow at two."

"They move fast, there can't be many applications."

"True. They say on the website the interview will be followed by a site visit, are we prepared for that ?"

"The boys have been in since yesterday afternoon re-enforcing that back wall so we can fit security on it, should be done by the end of the week."

"Excellent. I'll find out more tomorrow about what they want in place, and how far the licence extends, when I know you'll know."

"Jim I look forward to the call."

Jim grinned down the phone and gently hung up. Picturing the next day as the job interview to end all job interviews he decided to physically travel the route there and then, hoping to eliminate all possible surprises on the big day itself. Getting to South West London by train took him thirty-eight minutes, walking to the CLA building from the station took six minutes. He decided not to linger outside the building, no doubt they had cameras covering the outside and he wanted his appearance the following day to have the full force of a dramatic debut. Jim returned to the train station, noting the trip back only took him four minutes, the return train journey took an hour and a half.

Jim spent Tuesday night reviewing his paperwork. The man had supplied him with the lease to the shop and the financial records of the business that the CLA wished to see. Jim had them neatly filed with tabs arranged for swift access. Jim had his own CV, bank records, birth certificate and passport in the pockets of a leather document folder, he was satisfied he was prepared. He found himself heading to the bathroom mirror to check his appearance, realising on the way that clean shaven on a Tuesday night did not guarantee clean shaven on a Wednesday afternoon. Jim sighed admonishingly at the bathroom mirror. There was no more to be done but sleep was out of the question. Jim decided this really was time for a smoke, even if on medical grounds alone, he really must sleep in order to complete his preparation, a little subtle smoke would swiftly send him to the land of nod. Jim rolled a short stubby one and crouched by the window waving the smoke out into the night sky. He took a few moments to let the tetrahydrocannaboids roll around his brain, and confident the butt was fully out Jim curled up on his bed, he was asleep in seconds, whilst a breeze coming in through the open window gently spread the night spreading the contents of the ash tray across the carpet.

Wednesday morning arrived and Jim sprung to life. His eyes opened, his brain came on line and the first thought it transmitted to his consciousness, 'you've got a big meeting at two pm.' Jim leapt out of bed, checked his paperwork and document folder, cleaned the stain off the carpet, and switched on the laptop, it was six am. Jim referred to his brain as to what he should do next, 'No smoking' came the reply. This caused Jim to look across to his tin, his special little tin, 'I've got tobacco, I've got papers, I've got gear' his consciousness told him, 'and there's plenty of time until two.' Brain cut in, 'if you cannot control yourself at these crucial times you will not win.' Jim admonished his brain for being so unerringly sensible but couldn't deny that for once he was giving himself excellent advice. 'Exercise', suggested his brain ? 'It's that or madness,' replied his consciousness. Jim looked for his T-shirt and trainers, ten minutes later he was pounding resentfully around the park. There were two other joggers and a small number of dog walkers also out at the time, Jim ignored them all, he kept his eyes focused on the path ahead and his ears set to the sound of his footfalls. His brain tried to interrupt his exercise sending him thoughts such as, 'don't use up your energy', 'check the time', 'have you prepared for this meeting enough', following it with, 'is there any point to this, they're going to say no, you've left your job, what were you thinking, check the time again, now !' Jim tried to drown out his brain's bleating by running faster, it worked, but soon his lungs and feet began lodging their own complaints about what he was up to.

Jim slowed to a walk and allowed his brain voice. It continued to question his actions and recent decisions. He addressed his brain. 'I can't stop now' his consciousness informed it, 'so you coming out with all these worries and fears at this moment is really not helping.' His brain apologised and explained it was last minute nerves and the fact that it wasn't consulted before Jim had quit his job that had caused it concern. Jim did realise at that moment that maybe he hadn't quite thought things through, but his consciousness swiftly responded, 'well you wouldn't have acted if you did.' It went on to remind him of how he was before, living in fear of his lack of ambition, Jim grimaced knowingly in reaction to this thought. His brain and consciousness aligned, together they told him, you are in between the past and the future, so right now it's up to you. Jim nodded his acknowledgement, he resumed running, a jog quickly turned into a sprint and soon Jim was roaring full pelt down the park path yelling, "I should do this, I can do this, I will do this.' One of the dog walkers scooped up their pup and quickly left the park.

Jim returned home showered, and chose his attire. He selected the greyer of his two suits, a white shirt and a low-key monochrome tie. 'You are a dull and reliable shop keeper,' he told himself. He checked his papers and document folder for the final time, placed them both in a shoulder bag which he hung across his chest and secured it against his side with his left arm. It was now approaching twelve. Jim had decided based on the previous day's experience to allow two hours for the journey, he refused his brain's request to make any more suggestions, and marched out of the flat in the direction of the station. A train was pulling in just as he arrived, he was in South West London in twenty-five minutes.

Jim spent his bonus hour determinedly and viciously reading a newspaper in the coffee shop attached to the train station. Each article he read he attacked in the same way, 'occupy me, interest me,' he demanded of it, and when it failed to do so he mentally slagged off the individual or organisation being reported on, chastising them for whatever misfortune they had suffered. He knew this was pointless so Jim gave up on the broadsheet and picked up a tabloid instead. He found himself more at ease with a newspaper that was designed to be read briefly and found himself sufficiently occupied. After a second tabloid and third coffee the hour had passed.

Jim reached the CLA building in three minutes, it was now ten to two. Time had caught up with last night's ambition. He was ready, Jim strode purposefully up the steps and prepared to make his pitch.

In the lobby of the building Jim was greeted by a wall of glass. He could just make out that the receptionist was male but no details beyond that. A voice emerging from the sieve in front of him requested he provide two forms of identification. He opened his document wallet and pulled out his passport and a bank statement and slid them underneath the glass. Twenty seconds later they were slid back out and the disembodied voice asked him to go through a door to his right and take a seat. Jim found himself in an interview room which contained a desk and two chairs bolted to the floor, beyond that the room was bare except for miniscule black lenses attached to the four corners of the ceiling. Jim took the seat furthest from the door, laid his papers out on the desk in front of him, sat down and waited.

Sixty or so seconds later a middle-aged woman entered the room. Jim stood. The woman held out her hand and the two of them performed a polite nervous handshake. "Hello," she said, "I am a CLA official, you wish to make an application.."

"Yes I do," affirmed Jim, he indicated his paperwork on the desk, "I believe I have all the information you require."

"Excellent," replied the lady, "then let us begin." They each took their seats on the opposing sides of the table.

"Now the purpose of this interview is to ascertain if you will qualify for a licence to retail cannabis from prescribed premises within the United Kingdom."

Jim nodded his understanding.

"We will ascertain if you have the character and the resources to take on this highly responsible role."

Jim nodded gravely.

"If the licence is granted we will also carry out an on-going process of ensuring you are adhering to the rules we have put in place to ensure your customers are protected and safe-guarded to the greatest extent possible."

"I understand."

The lady stared intently at Jim, he stared dolefully back.

"Our first question Mr Pemberton is why. Why do you wish to sell drugs to the British public ?"

"I wish to make a profit. I want to provide a service the dope smokers of the UK don't currently receive. I want to offer good quality marijuana from a set place that is open at set hours, and with those safe-guarding rules firmly in place," Jim hurriedly added.

The official acknowledged Jim's reply with a sigh, "and you are aware that smoking in general, and particularly smoking cannabis is harmful to people's health.."

"I am aware that it is in the long term, certainly. Equally alcohol, gambling and debt are also available to the British public and all of these are far more damaging to the individual. I get the impression that by legalising the cannabis trade the government hopes to be able limit the damage that dope smokers are doing to themselves, and I am very happy to be a part of that process."

The answer appeared to satisfy the official.

"You are quite right Mr Pemberton. Alas yes many people do insist upon taking courses of action that are harmful to themselves, that seems unpreventable. What the government does wish to prevent is drug dealers hanging around outside school gates, and the shocking rise in the number of young people experiencing mental health problems stemming from cannabis consumption. We hope by legalising the trade, we are setting the permitted age for your customers at twenty-one by the way, we really can protect the young and vulnerable in society."

"I understand," replied Jim truthfully, "and if granted a licence I do promise there will be no sales campaigns, no marketing, I will run a quiet little shop for adults only."

"Good Mr Pemberton, now are you qualified ?"

"I have been running a shop, a secure shop, a jewellers, for ten years, I believe I have the experience."

"We will be checking that with your former employers."

"No problem."

"Now I see that you have obtained premises, a former vape shop in Croydon."

“I have, and we are fully prepared to implement any further security features that are required.”

“There will be.”

“May I ask a question ?”

“You may ?”

“Regarding the growing of the plants, must this take place on the premises too ?”

“The anti-drug laws are still in place Mr Pemberton, we need them so we have a reason to arrest illicit drug dealers. The cultivation and selling of cannabis will remain illegal, except on licensed premises.”

“Then surely my customers will be breaking the law as soon as they leave the shop ?”

“The product you distribute will be clearly stamped and identified as having been issued by a licenced dealer, this will be a defence should your customers come into contact with the police.”

Jim looked quizzical.

“So people can still be arrested ?”

“That is the case.”

“So it’s not really full legalisation..”

“Correct Mr Pemberton it is not. The government is engaged in a programme of limited licencing of the activity, they have not granted full permission for marijuana to be consumed anywhere and everywhere.”

“I get that, but if there’s a danger my suppliers and customers maybe arrested at any moment that does present a certain amount of difficulty in running a business.”

“It is not an easy path you are choosing Mr Pemberton, yes that is a difficulty that you will have to face. However although the local police will be aware of your shop’s existence, I have been informed they will not specifically target any licensed shop or its’ customers.”

“That’s a relief.”

“This is a new venture for British society Mr Pemberton, there will be a deal of great public interest in how the situation develops.”

“Absolutely, what’s the next step ?”

“Well having had this interview I am happy to let your application proceed. We will now begin the process of checking your references and referees, Mr Pemberton we will be in touch.”

The official stood, Jim stood, they shook hands once more, Jim gathered up his papers and carefully left the room. He nodded to the sieve as he left and walked sedately down the steps of the building and out onto the street, once he had turned the corner he gripped his right hand into a fist and fiercely punched the air. “Yes !” He shouted out to no-one in particular, and continued his walk with an enormous smile on his face, he made the station in two minutes.

“The shop will be legit, supplying it and buying from it remains illegal,” Jim told the man in a phone call later that day.

“You what !? Well how’s that going to work ?”

“They told me the police won’t be targeting our customers.”

“Well that’s mighty agreeable of them.”

“We’ve got this far, we keep going, do you think you can arrange supply ?”

“Jim I’ve got seeds in from Amsterdam, I’ve got houses and warehouses full of plants hidden all over this great city. I have plans, back-up plans and back-up back-up plans, I can supply.”

“Brilliant ! Well they’re checking me out as we speak, once that’s done it’ll be the site visit.”

“The boys are still there working, they’re gonna make the partition wall, knife proof, flame proof and bullet proof, I mean to protect my investment.”

“Nice, secure is nice.”

“Damn right, you given any thought to staff, you can’t be there all the time.”

“What about the guy that was running the shop before ?”

“Nah, too flakey, you find some people, some people you trust.”

“Will do,” said Jim confidently as he hung up.” ‘How’ his brain retorted, ‘add in the paper, shop assistants required for dope shop, that will not find you the right type of person.’ Jim agreed with his brain, his consciousness took over, this is a dilemma that needs to be resolved with good drink and smart conversation, Jim texted Rob.

Clink.

Rob's face was a perfect picture of anticipation. "So did they say yes ?" He blurted out.

"They're checking on me as we speak. I've got premises, a vape shop in Croydon.."

"Croydon !?" Interrupted Rob.

"Croydon." Repeated Jim. "If the licence is granted we're good to go."

"Oh man that is so ..epic !"

"It feels good mate, it really does, to be going above and beyond what I'm used to, what can I say other than, well here we go !"

Clink.

"What about yourself, seen your wife lately ?"

"Oh not for.." Rob checked his watch, "about six months now."

"Still going well then ?"

"Well we've not split up, at least not that her lawyer has told me, and he drinks in here, I think she's still assessing the situation."

"Well I don't know why she can't see that you're a top bloke, who has given her and will continue to give her a great life."

"Yeah in my rented flat above a kebab shop and next to a night club."

"Still not found anywhere better ?"

"Don't want to, the landlord gives me a discount on the rent for mopping the sick up off the pavement each morning."

"Er yeah, ee-zee money."

"That coupled with a few odd jobs sees me good for rent, food and weed."

"If you had a regular income would that help ?"

"What you saying mate ?"

"I trust you Rob and that counts for a lot. I need people I can trust to work in the shop, would you consider it ?"

"Aw man, I mean I will be your number one customer when you're up and running, but working there," Rob blew a lengthy blast of air from between his teeth, " think about it, you're going to be supplying the underworld with their gear and the overworld with their drug of choice yah. Things are going to get messy, mate, are you prepared for that ?"

"The man is having a bullet proof wall built behind the counter."

"Yeah but what about the guy with a knife in front of the counter ?"

"Gotta be charming and disarming, which you are !"

"Jim.."

"Listen the CLA are going to insist on a number of security features which we will do, staff safety is vitally important, I'm staff too ! But when I'm not there I need someone I trust who will be honest with the money and honest with the dope."

Rob, indecision filling his eyes, looked at Jim long and hard.

"Staff discount."

"I'm in."

Clink.

"Okay so don't go quitting your jobs just yet, the licence still has to be approved, but once that's done I want you there mate from day one, please."

Clink.

Jim received a phone call from the CLA that Friday, they confirmed that he had been personally approved as a potential licensee and arrangements were made to conduct the site visit the following Monday. It was explained that the visit would be conducted by two CLA officials, a local neighbourhood police officer and a representative of Croydon council, Jim was clearly warned that all parties must be satisfied before the license was granted. Jim rang the man and arranged to meet him at the shop on the Saturday to check over the premises in advance.

They pair met outside the shop and the man greeted Jim with a warm hug, “so we good ?” “So far so good,” replied Jim, “next hurdle, Monday, and by the way the visit is going to be by the CLA, council and police.” “Have fun !” retorted the man handing Jim the shop keys. “You’re not…” “Can’t have contact with the police man, little matter of an outstanding warrant.” Jim looked pensive. “Jim, my friend, as you said yourself, you are the acceptable face of this operation, if those folks see my face they’re suddenly going to come up with a lot more questions.”

“Yes but..”

“Jim first you were concerned about the money, did they ask you where it was coming from ?”

“No they did not,” recalled Jim.

“There you go, people don’t care where the money’s coming from, they just want to know you’ve got it. And if they ask you about the supply, they don’t really want to know, they just need to know you can, and with me behind you, you can. You’ll be fine, you know it, so let me show you the improvements, it’s the key with the blue sticker.”

Jim let them both into the shop, the false wall behind the counter had been replaced with a wall of breeze blocks, inset into which was a wooden door rimmed with silver metal.

“Get behind that and you’ll be safe,” boasted the man. Jim slapped the wall in a mock attempt to batter through it, “hope so,” he replied. “Definitely so,” responded the man. “Okay, good we’ve got something solid to show them on Monday.”

The Monday morning meeting began as expected. The CLA officials had made a clear effort to appear as bland as possible. One was male, one was female, both business-suited, no name badges. The Croydon council official wore glasses. He had a hooked nose to rest them on, and in the first few seconds of meeting him it became apparent he had a problem with his depth perception. The local neighbourhood police officer was not a local neighbourhood police officer at all, he wore a white shirt not a blue one and had an array of silver emblems on his shoulders. Jim gathered everyone inside the shop, the policeman spoke first.

"So this is where it will be huh ? Oh well Good Luck, but don't expect my officers to come running every single time someone comes in here brandishing a weapon, let's be realistic, this is Croydon, your little social experiment here is all well and good, but it's my job to keep the peace, I think it's fair to say we can appreciate that there may well be a serious risk of disorder at this venue." The policeman turned to the council officer, "what's the budget ?"

"Oh no budget at all," replied the council officer, "it's just another licensed premises." The council officer turned to Jim, "I would recommend you join shopwatch, our scheme connected to local security officers employed and monitored by the council, however Croydon council doesn't see why it should suffer any financial impediment just because of what central government has decided to authorise." The council official turned to the CLA officials, walked two feet forward to bring them into focus, and squinted hard at the bureaucrats from South West London.

The female CLAian looked at the male CLAian, the male looked back at the female, the female raised an eyebrow and pointed her lips in the direction of the bureaucrat from South London. The male spoke.

"Well first I must make it clear that we have yet to grant these premises and this gentleman a licence. The whole purpose of this visit is to see if both are suitable, and of course ascertain the attitudes of the local authority and the local police, both of which are extremely pertinent to the granting of the licence. You have said Sir that the council is keen not to suffer any financial loss due to these premises being located within this borough, does the council have any other objections may I ask ?"

"Well we don't seem to have any choice about it do we. If the law has been amended to allow the distribution of cannabis from licensed properties, and you have decided to grant a licence to someone located here, well there's not a lot we can do about it is there, but we're not paying for it !"

"Objection duly noted," spoke the female CLAian. She turned to the policeman, "and you, Chief Inspector, can you summarise the attitude of the local police ?"

"Well I'm not thick enough to see there can't be benefits. Take the drugs trade off the streets, bring it into legal establishments like this, now that could be a seriously big reduction to our workload. However, like a gem store, bank, or electrical shop, this particular retail outlet is highly likely to be targeted by some serious 'oodlums, that is my most serious and present concern, so I'll tell you what I would want for a start, bollards !"

"Bollards..." Countered the female CLAian.

"Bollards." Repeated the policeman. "Let's face it the little shits will at some point attempt to ram raid this shop. I want proper bollards, concrete wrapped around steel, dug into the pavement immediately outside the premises, plus it'll stop all your stoned customers wandering out into the road."

"No." Interjected the female CLAian, "We cannot and do not authorise the consumption of cannabis on the premises. It is a major part of the licence that cannabis cannot be consumed, smoked or eaten on the premises. The licence is only for the selling and distribution of the product, is that clear ?"

"Utterly clear and understood," piped up Jim.

"We do also insist on the security arrangements being to the satisfaction of the local police and so if bollards is the suggestion, then bollards it must be."

"We're not paying," said the Croydon official.

"What is the cost of bollards ?" inquired Jim.

"You won't see change from five figures," suggested the policeman.

Jim turned to face the Croydon official, the official adjusted his stance to focus on Jim in return, "If I arrange payment can the council place the bollards ?"

"That should be possible" muttered the official.

"Then I will," stated Jim and he turned to face the CLA couple.

"What other conditions do I need to satisfy ?"

"This is the security system we wish you to apply. As stated the minimum age for purchase is twenty-one, and Mr Pemberton, we really want that limit to be enforced. This is not like cigarettes, this is not like fireworks, we want this to work. So how it's done…" The female CLA official waggled her fore finger in the air, "finger scan and the presentation of photo ID. Every customer must pre-register, at that time they will show you their passport, plus one other form of photo ID, though we didn't think a driving licence was quite appropriate, and their finger will be scanned at that time. They then must provide a matching finger scan and one form of identification at each future purchase. The quantity of each purchase will be limited to seven point zero eight seven grammes, or a quarter of an ounce, purchases will be date and time stamped, providing evidence of where they were sourced," the official nodded to the policeman, "and purchases will be limited to one every seventy-two hours."

"Wow, you've really thought this through.." countered Jim.

"We're allowing it not encouraging it," replied the male official. "These rules will be enforced, we will be providing the technology to make it possible, and we will be making sure it's used correctly. Small amounts, to adults is what's being permitted."

"And I will be happy to be the legal supplier, " smiled Jim.

“Our equipment will be bolted into place on the front counter, what other security arrangements will you have in place ?”

“My thoughts are we will have two SIA licenced gents at the door at all times for the first two weeks we’re open, just until the initial excitement dies down. They will be there to bolt the door if they see anyone approaching brandishing a weapon, and herd any time wasters from the shop. Should any assailants get passed them, they and the shop assistants will get behind this wall here,“ Jim slapped the breeze blocks, ”and if it has come to that if we might please be permitted a call to the police at that time..”

The chief inspector growled.

“And have you considered what the affect may be on the local community ?” Interjected the Croydon official.

“Negligible. Strictly no consumption on premises as has been said, though hopefully an increased number of shoppers visiting the area will lead to a positive knock-on effect for local businesses. I guarantee they’ll be battling it out to set up a snack shop next door !”

The Croydon official pursed his lips and set about adjusting the position of his glasses.

“Well then,” led the female CLA official ,”when such security arrangements as described here today have been put in place, you may open. It would seem as if you and Croydon council have an installation to arrange..”

“Good day to you all,” the police officer left the shop.

The male CLA official spoke, “please contact us Mr Pemberton so we can have people come and install the security scanner and registration machine, a thank you to you all for your time.” The officials from the CLA smiled politely and quietly left the shop. The Croydon council representative held a business card up a foot in front of Jim’s face. “This is how to contact me.” Jim took the card from the official, who turned, identified to himself where the door was and then bustled his way out of the shop.

Jim watched him make his way down the street. He was alone, he went over what had been said, he walked behind the counter of what he knew now was going to be his shop. He turned to face his future customers. “Yeah !” he roared ! Both fists, equidistant in the air. “Roll up, roll up, roll up, come and get it, the first and only legal marijuana shop in the UK ! We have what you want.” Jim looked across his counter and guided his future customers towards his future wares.

Jim needed to share his feelings. In a moment his mobile was in his hand, a call rather than a text suggested his brain, his fingers obeyed and he rang Rob.

“Mate.”

“Mate.”

“You got the licence didn’t you.”

“I did mate I did.”

“Oh yes.”

“So you want the job mate ?”

“You know what, yes I do.”

“You sure.”

“I’m sure”

“We should drink.”

“Where are you ?”

“In Croydon.”

“You come to me.”

Jim and Rob settled on Clapham and each arrived half an hour after the call was made. They located an empty unpleasant bar across from the station, ordered their pints and clinked away.

"Oh this is going to be good, so damn good."

"This is going to be intense, just like carry on camping, there are going to be so many kids turning up with fake ID it'll be unreal, how are you, we, going to deal with it ?"

"We won't have to, the CLA will be providing us with the technology, all customers have to present a passport plus other ID to pre-register.."

"What if they've got hold of a fake passport.."

"If someone can fake a passport I reckon there'll do more with that than registering at a dope shop."

"Mmm."

"And when they register they have to provide a finger scan, and then again for each future purchase, which are limited to one every three days by the way, so it's ID and finger scan each time, and it's over twenty-ones only, looks like the government has actually thought this thing through."

"Excellent ! But what about the protests from the mothers' groups, the puritans and the religious zealots ?"

"We'll be legal man, if they start picketing, we can call the police for protection."

"Mmm"

"Come on man, why so nervous, this is opportunity staring us in the face."

" 'cause man, you know, this country, occasionally yes it has ideas, then it gets all nervous and votes conservative."

"Yes but they've taken my money and given me a license, a licence to thrill baby !"

"They could rescind the licence."

"The government rip me off.... They wouldn't dare, it'd destroy faith in the system, there'd be riots."

"Hey this is dope smokers we're talking about, there'd be sit ins, lots and lots of really really low down sit ins."

Jim and Rob laughed.

Rob continued, “but seriously man, they the government, the state, do hold the power, if they chose they could stand in the way.”

“They’ve got me cash they’ve given me the authorisation, and when they see the tax money rolling in and the local council sees the incredible increase in trade around the area, I’m confident they’ll be quietly onside, I have to be. Money makes the world go around, dope makes that more palatable.”

“Dude you have the slogan ! So what’s next ?”

“Bollards.”

“Bollards to you too, I asked what’s next ?”

“Installing bollards outside the shop, it’s what the police insisted on.”

“Croydon” the guys muttered simultaneously.

III. The Opening

The erection of the bollards took place surprisingly quickly, Croydon council swiftly despatched three silent aggressive men, led by a bombastic man of many words, who arrived in two flatbed trucks at the premises now known as Legal Jims.

“Right”, said the man of many words “now a bollard is a most magnificent thing, solid, upwardly thrusting, reliable, a permanent piece of street furniture, now your retractable bollard, well that’s even better, does the whole solid upwardly thrusting thing, yet can be discretely withdrawn at anytime.. we will not be using retractable bollards in this instance, there is no time of day that the local residents of this fair borough will not consider driving a nicked motor through the front of your shop to be a good idea. So we is going to erect four permanent bollards at the edge of your pavement see, we’re gonna dig down three feet, make a beautiful hole, into which we’ll be pouring only the most fragrant and aromatic concrete, which we will be reinforcing with twisted metal, steel mesh, iron prongs, until we have filled that hole of three feet and then continued to rise to a height of three feet above the pavement and you will have four permanent sentries, guardsmen, protectors on duty outside your shop everyday and every night.”

“Please excuse me while I wipe a tear from my eye in contemplation of the beautiful erections you will shortly install, would the process be enhanced by my going into the shop and putting the kettle on ?..”

That it would my man, that it would, two sugars, two sugars, no sugars, four sugars !”

“Coming up !”

Jim entered the shop smiling and reached for his mobile, the man was still listed as ‘unknown number’, Jim called the unknown.

“Wah Gwaan !”

“Bollards being erected as we speak, oh and second staff member secured, the CLA wishes to deliver us their security machines on Monday, and train us in their operation, so next week, when that’s complete Legal Jims can open its’ doors!”

“Ya mon, let’s get London stoned !”

Deep within the bowels of the CLA building an electrical device was being prepared. A female engineer clicked down its' lid and turned to her male counterpart.

"There it's complete, it does require a first test subject, just so we know it's capable of recording a persons' details, would you oblige.."

"Have my details on that database, not bloody likely. Let's get one of the interior designers."

The engineer smiled and the male rose from his chair, crossed to the door and opening it called out, "Darling would you mind coming in here a moment, just need to borrow you for something." The interior designer duly obliged and entered the room, the male continued, "it's our identity scanner thingy, making sure we can tie up a fingerprint with a person, please if you could just pop your finger in there" "Oh okay" responded the interior designer, who checked their nail then placed their finger on the scanner. The machine shone a bright blue light over the finger and a moment late an image of the fingerprint appeared on the device's screen, that image was swiftly replaced by an image containing a picture and details of the interior designer and following that the screen was covered by a pulsating green tick.

"Excellent" smiled the engineer handing back the interior designer back their finger, "and I am confident if you were under twenty-one that green tick would have been a flashing red cross, thanks so much for your help." The interior designer smiled and left the room in a bemused state.

The engineer turned to her colleague.

"So there we go, fingerprint and identity confirmed for every purchase. Used honestly this system will prevent young persons and undesirables making purchases"

"And will record the identity of everyone buying cannabis."

"And" countered the engineer whilst holding up a gold-plated cat six cable, "this is the link that will bring all that information straight back to us."

On Monday morning Jim and Rob awaited the arrival of the installers from the Cannabis Licensing Authority. Each of them had chosen to wear a polo shirt and clean jeans, their hair was brushed and neither of them was stoned. As they waited each began regarding the other's appearance, Rob began the conversation.

"You know we should get a uniform, present a standard front."

"I agree with that," replied Jim.

Rob continued his contemplations, "..but no name tags.."

"Definitely not name tags." Affirmed Jim.

"We could do utility belts ?.."

"Utility belts ?.."

"You know, with things hanging off them, tools, pouches, keys.. shark-repellant spray."

"Don't think it should be limited to just sharks."

"Aye we should repel without prejudice."

But.. Almost seriously, we could do belts, with stuff on 'em, like extendable batons and stuff."

"Jim there's laws about carrying weapons and stuff and when it comes down to it I'm a lover not a fighter. You said the man would provide two security guys on the door for the first couple of weeks."

"Uh huh"

"That'll do me, no need for us to get tooled up, but I wouldn't mind looking as if I was tooled up."

"Mmm."

"Well okay howabout not belts, but pockets, big deep mysterious pockets, I'm thinking long brown coats.."

"Like proper hardware store brown coats" said Jim nodding.

"Just like proper hardware store brown coats !" Nodded Rob emphatically.

Jim turned his attention to the lap top sitting on the counter, “I’m thinking used rather than new, unless you want to go boutique. So there’s you, me, the man, and there could well be more staff in the future and if we want everyone to look standard.

“Or buy new and scuff ‘em up. Hey each new member of staff gets to mess them up in their own particular way.”

“Right, that right there is company policy. Now what do you call ‘em ? Store coats ?”

There was a knock at the door.

Rob answered the door, it was the female CLA engineer, two non-descript men stood behind her carrying a non-descript box.

“Customer registration and payment facilitation equipment ?”

“Nah you want the take-away next door”

The engineer processed the statement, she did not have the wrong address, she had double checked it, the man was smiling, this was possibly an attempt at humour.

Rob could only bare her quizzical look so much and felt compelled to interrupt it with “yes, yes, yes, you’re from the CLA right ?”

Rob threw open the door and welcomed the three persons into the shop. Jim stood behind the counter gesturing with both hands as to where the customer registration and payment facilitation equipment should be placed. The non-descript men duly carried the bland box to the indicated location. The engineer looked at Rob and clearly decided against saying anything further to him, she went and stood directly in front of Jim.

“You are Mr James Pemberton ? ”

“I am Mr James Pemberton.” “And these are the premises of Legal Jims.”

The engineer acknowledged the statements.

“This must be the customer registration and payment facilitation equipment.”

The engineer acknowledged.

“As requested there’s a steel frame work for it to be bolted to.”

Jim indicated behind the wooden counter within which a lattice of metal had been bolted to the concrete shop floor, four bore holes through the top of counter allowed the connection of the equipment to the lattice. The non-descript men set to work.

“Right.” Announced the engineer.

Rob rushed to Jim’s side and the two stood to attention.

Rob rushed to Jim’s side and the two stood to attention.

“This has been explained before I believe..” Jim nodded, Rob stuttered. “But I will repeat it for clarity. This equipment both registers your customers and works as your till. Unless a person is registered as a customer they cannot make a purchase. To register as a customer they will have to provide two forms of printed identification and allow their finger to be scanned at that point. Hence you gentlemen, or rather your machine will have access to some databases to which the public does not normally have access, they’ll be the electoral register, NDDNA, PNC, also some financial databases to check the payment is legitimate and it also connects with a medical database, we do not think it a good idea that you sell to people with a history of cannabis induced psychosis…”

“Oh agreed” nodded Rob and Jim.

“So will this machine end up rejecting a lot of people ?” Inquired Rob.

“The only grounds the machine will reject customers on is if they are less than twenty-one years of age at the time of registration, not a legitimate UK citizen, or on medical grounds. You also have the ability to refuse a customer registration, regardless of whether or not they are accepted onto the database.”

“We can ‘just say no’…” floated Rob.

“Yes. Each registered customer can make a purchase of seven point zero eight seven grammes every seventy-two hours.”

“A quarter every three days.”

“They do not have to purchase the maximum amount, you will be using scales I presume..”

Nodding.

“Then you simply record whatever weight and at what cost you have made the sale here, the computer will add the when, and that will determine the time at which that customer can make the next purchase.”

“Simples.”

The non-descript men finished their bolting and took a power cable and a golden cat six cable from the back of the machine and plugged them into their relevant sockets. The equipment announced its’ sentience with a recurring beep. The screen flashed, the engineer motioned that Jim, Rob and the non-descript men should all look away while she entered a password. Jim and Rob heard a few keyboard taps behind them, followed by a low whistle from the engineer and then the sound of firm tap on a large button.

“There.” Announced the engineer. Jim and Ron turned and she presented them with a screen awaiting the entry of a customer‘s details. “That is the finger scanner, documents can be scanned or the details entered via the keyboard, and you gentlemen are now ready to start selling.”

“Thank you” replied Jim.

The engineer nodded to Jim, then Rob, then performed a different nod to the non-descript men. They didn’t nod a response, instead they turned to each other and checked between themselves that they’d gathered up all the remains of the non-descript box and then quietly left the shop followed moments later by the engineer.

Jim smiled a 'that's a job done' smile, Rob's smile was one of bemusement. Rob shook his head and turned inquisitively towards Jim. Jim already had his phone dialling out and was raising it to his ear.

The man's "aaaaaaahh…" rang through the shop.

"Hey man," replied Jim, "it's time to stock the shop."

"On my way."

As Jim and Rob were familiarising themselves with the machinery the man strolled in through the back of the shop.

His eyes were masked by sunglasses but the smile was clear to see. He perused the wooden counter and the small wooden drawers stacked up on the wall behind it with a proprietorial air. His elbows catapulted outwards and his hands grabbed his hip bones.

"Ooh yes…"

His head slowly moved along the drawers from left to right, and then back again, as he started on a third traverse Rob spoke up.

"There's thirty two of them. And they delivered the till this morning, we're good to go when.."

The man held up his finger. Rob stopped speaking, Jim did not start.

"Gentlemen…"

The man kept his finger in the air and swivelled one hundred and eighty degrees on the ball of his right foot landed smoothly and strode for the door, grabbed it and held it open.

"Gentlemen."

Jim and Rob realised they should follow, they passed through the open door, the man swivelled out behind them and lent against one of the bollards. He lit a cigarillo with a match and he took his time about it. Rob and Jim watched on in silence, in front of them a car detached itself from the traffic and pulled up by the end bollard, the window whirred down and two young black lads looked out with apprehensive confidence, the passenger turned to the man, the man nodded to Jim and Rob, Rob leant forward and was handed a package, he looked confusedly towards Jim, Jim eyes indicated he should take the package inside sharpish, Rob snapped to it, the window whirred up and the car sped off.

As Rob returned to the street a second car arrived, an estate family model, and the window rolled down to reveal a lady who was clearly somebody's mum. She waved at the man and spoke out in a sing-song voice, "Oh hi Donny, got your package."

"Knew you would beautiful" replied the man in his deepest tones, and indicated that Jim should take the package from the mum.

"Thank you" he said cheerily before taking the package and handing it to Rob.

The next car contained two over enthusiastic young white lads, the furtive one in the passenger seat leaned out of the window and hissed, "Right time and place yeah Johnny ?"

"Right time and place" responded the man in tired tones.

The furtive lad handed his package to Rob with a theatrical wink, Rob took the package inside.

The next car was red and sporty and driven by a beautiful woman. She chose to park her car further down the road and walk back to where Jim, Rob and the Man were standing. They were very glad she did. She sidled up to the man and purred, "got your package Johnny". The man exhaled smoke and turned his head to Rob, the beautiful woman held out the package, Rob took it without eye contact being made, the woman turned, slowly, and then walked back to her car, nothing was said. Rob tried to speak but his jaw didn't work. He held up the package and motioned feebly that he would take it into the shop. Another car pulled up, a shiny expensive model, a well-dressed black guy held out a package, no-one looked at him, they were fixated as the beautiful woman poised herself to get back into her car. The well-dressed black guy poked his head out, appraised the scene, took Jim's limp fingers and squeezed them around the package, and drove away laughing.

"Five."

The man sighed.

"We've got five packages. Is that all of them ?"

"I've got two more on stand-by… standing by, but looks like everyone got through. Let's stock the shop."

"Yes let's do that" muttered Jim meekly following the man into the shop.

On the counter lay the five packages, each a little larger than a shoe box and wrapped densely in brown plastic tape, seemingly with the intent that no odour should escape from within. The man laid the five packages out side by side. "Now !..." Announced the man. "These five packages probably all look like shoe boxes containing dope… and that's because they are all shoe boxes containing dope. Tightly-packed dope stored and sorted in a way that we do not want to damage. So please gentlemen when you take your blade.." The man's key-ring contained a flick-knife, Jim reached for a stanley knife, Rob grabbed a pair of scissors. "Will you please run that blade in from the side and stop when you reach hard cardboard." The man proceeded to slice around the sides of the first package so the lid could be popped off. Jim and Rob did the same and finishing first each proceeded to take the top of a second package, with the lids cut from all five boxes the men flipped them all open.

The aromas erupted. Spices, herbs, flowers, all joyfully released their spores into the air space above the counter. Jim breathed in, the man breathed in, Rob breathed in, Rob lost his footing and steadied himself against the back wall. The air sparkled with the smell of cannabis, Rob regained his footing and the three men stood there, smiling at each other.

The man removed his sunglasses, his eyes were full of tears. "Boys" he declared, "I think this could be the start of something beautiful."

Jim, Rob and the man stood around the packages and admired them.

Time passed.

More time passed.

It carried on like this for a while.

"We should stock the shelves" one of them murmured.

A different segment of time passed.

The voice was heard again.

"We really should stock the shelves."

This time there was a reply, "yes, yes we should."

The men looked up at each other and smiled, the need for a job of work to be done permeated their collective minds, the lips drooped and seriousness infected their eyebrows, "Okay how do we categorise this ?" Asked Jim.

"Well…." Began the man, "tradition states that we divide along the lines of Indica and Sativa, now let us go alphabetical and place Indica on the left and Sativa on the right. So Indica, as originating from the Hindu Kush mountains of India don't you know…" The man's voice took on a teacher's tone, "and Indica includes purple kush, bubba kush, granddaddy purple, afghan kush and.. Northern Lights." The man took the quarter ounce packages and placed them in the drawers to the left of the doorway. With the Northern Lights he paused and smiled, pulled open a pack and inhaled the smell so fully and completely that for a moment all motion stopped whilst Rob and Jim simply stared at the man breathing it in. "Northern Lights, " he purred, "where it all began for me." Motion returned and the man swept to the right of the doorway, "now here on the Sativa side we'll put Acapulco Gold Maui Waui and a little Supernatural. After that so many of these strains are hybrids and crossovers we may as well just go alphabetical, now we have five thousand seven point zero eight seven gram baggies in these boxes, and those folks that dropped these off this morning, well they're all headed off to prepare some more, gentlemen we have stock and we have supply."

Rob went to stand by the till, "we have method of registration and payment" he reported.

Jim looked over the shop islands of bongs, pipes, papers and then on towards the door. "And we're legal and we're ready to open."

Rob chipped in, "you know we really should have thought of like advertising and promotion and stuff…"

"Gentlemen please." Interjected the man, he walked over to the display stand and took the sturdiest looking bong and largest pipe he could see and walked out the shop door, swiftly followed by Jim and Rob. The man strode between the bollards and into the middle of the street and stopped. He raised the bong above his head with his right hand and tapped against it the pipe in his left hand, gradually increasing the sound until he had created a resounding chime that echoed off the surrounding buildings, in the silence that followed the man spoke.

“People of Croydon here this. You can now legally buy schmoke ! The shop is right here. You must be over twenty-one, you must register, so if that’s you have we got dope for you ! The shop is now open.”

The man ceased his chiming, a car stopped and a window whirred down, curtains twitched across the road, the chef came out of the takeaway. Jim and Rob nodded their approval. “Well that’s the advertising taken care of,” smiled the man and the three men slipped back into the shop.

A young black man entered the shop. He looked across the display stands at the three men standing behind the counter, they looked back at him, he looked back at them. “So…” the young man began, ” I can walk in here and legally buy dope ?..”

Jim replied, “yes, you can.”

“If” interjected the man, “you are over twenty-one and can provide two forms of ID. Passport..”

“Or driving licence..” added Jim, “they relented, so it’s any two forms of identification, passport, licence, bill and your finger scanned here.”

The young man made a decision to trust Jim, The Man and Rob and walked to the counter.

“Okay I’m game” he said and produced a wallet from his left trouser pocket and his index finger from his right pocket. Using his index finger first he browsed and selected an ID card from the wallet which he gave to Rob who got typing, then he presented his finger to Jim who gently guided it into the scanner, a blue light rolled down the length of his finger print and having rolled back up it then extinguished itself politely.

“Right” said Rob “You are actually our…” surprised by what he saw on the screen Rob interrupted himself, “second customer.. there must be like an example customer number one, but you are our first physical customer in this shop, the computer accepts you are who you say you are, your payment card is registered on the system, what would you like mate ?”

The young man lent back and perused the titles etched on the draws lining the back wall. A smile burst over his face as he silently read out the names.

“And your stuff is… “

“Is the shit.” stated the man.

“Okay” nodded the customer “...pleeeasse make it Acapulco Gold”

“Coming right up !” Rob swivelled swiftly upon his ankles and took from a draw a quarter of acapulco gold and slid the bag into a section of the CLA registration machine where it was swiftly stamped and he brought the bag up to show the customer, “that sir is your cust ID, that is your product, please note the time stamp, you must wait seventy-two hours before making another purchase, and that there is your legally bought guilt–free bag of dope ”

The customer brought up both his hands to receive the dope, Rob proffered the dope with both of his hands, their hands met and clasped together in joyous rapture as they lifted the transparent plastic bag of reddish green herbs up before their eyes where together they could truly behold its’ wonder. The man came and joined Rob and the customer within the state of awe, he began speaking softly, “Gentlemen you have before you the first legal opiate to be sold in this country for one hundred and ten years ! My son, when you take this home and schmoke it you will be doing what generations and generations of tokers, smokers and jokers have been unable to do for over a century, you will be enjoying a legal smoke in England, Now you go home and you smoke this weed son, smoke it for yourself, and smoke it for all the dreams of all those who have smoked before you !”

The customer remained silent. He looked at the man, the man looked back, they hugged. He looked at Rob, Rob looked back, they hugged. The customer held up his precious purchase between them, they all beheld it and they smiled, the customer turned and made his way out of the shop, he skipped as he crossed the threshold. His exit was immediately followed by the entrance of the chef from the next door takeaway. The cook nervously approached the counter. His body language did all the talking so Rob swiftly replied, “Yes. Yes you can, you can legally come in here and buy cannabis, all you need is ID and a finger.” The cook held up a finger wrapped in a blue plaster. “We’ll find a way” murmured Rob as he ushered him in the direction of the CLA machine.

Rob gently explained to the chef, "it doesn't matter which finger you use, as long as you bring the same finger back with you next time, are you planning to cut any of your other fingers ?" The chef smiled and shook his head. The man spoke to Jim. "Two hours." Jim raised an eyebrow. "Two hours at the most, for that boy to go home, skin up and enjoy the finest spliff he's ever smoked in his life, which he will then just have to tell his mates about and then we'll have queues around the block." Jim nodded. "Those two big fuckers I mentioned, it's time for me to make a call." As the man slipped out the back and Rob served the customer and while Jim waited for the next one his own brain grabbed his attention for a moment, 'you know' it whispered to him, 'these are the right people, this is the right place and time, this was the right thing to do, just thought you should hear that' 'oh thanks brain, much appreciated' replied Jim.

The next customer did not prove to be the next customer, she was an excited teenage girl, Jim guessed at seventeen but he knew from seeing the looks his niece Imogen and her friends pulled off she really could be any age from twelve up, but he knew just nowhere near twenty-one.

"Oi Mister can you buy dope here legally !?"

"No Miss, not until you are twenty-one"

"Yeah well I am."

"No you are not."

"Wanker !"

The child left the shop.

The next customer was bearded and walked with a cane, though clearly a little unsure of his etiquette, he began..

"You know a little bird just told me.."

"It's all true" smiled Jim.

The elderly man triangulated his way towards the counter, cane first, path-finding its' way to a secure point, each leg then swung round to a position so that his legs balanced his body, then out with the cane again. As he rotated his way to the counter Jim put out a chair for him to rest on when he reached his destination. He sunk gratefully into it breathing out a thank you and having caught his breath looked up at Jim, Rob and the man. They waited for him to speak.

“Now Boys as you can imagine I suffer from quite a bit of pain in the legs.”

The boys nodded.

“And I’m told your stuff does quite a good job of easing pain.”

The boys nodded.

“Oo good only I’m not so sure I’m that adept at rolling.” The elderly man held up his elderly fingers.

“Oh well there’s always baking..” countered Rob.

“Ooh no that’s the wife’s area of the house, but I’ve always enjoyed a good cigar, and we have a balcony for the very purpose, it’s just..” the man raised his hands again with an “oh dear”.

The man was putting his phone away having sent a text, he stepped forward, “Sir we’ve got you covered.” The customer, Jim and Rob all paused in anticipation. “ Now if it’s pain relief you’re after may I suggest a lemon haze, known for its’ soothing qualities, here..” The man grabbed a quarter of the herb from the relevant drawer and popped open the bag in front of the customer who breathed it in deeply, a smile crossed his face.

“Ooh rather pungent isn’t it” he commented.

“All the flavours of the orient” smiled the man, “Rob if you’ll do the honours registering the gentleman, I must just check on something. While Rob helped the man position his finger appropriately the man swept to the door of the shop, looked out, clearly saw what he wanted to see and returned to the counter. They waited as Rob entered the details the system and payment was made and a sticker produced. The two young black lads who had delivered the first package came in to the shop and walked up to the man, he addressed both them and the customer, who’s registration had revealed his name to be Graham. “Now lads this is Graham,” all parties nodded, ”He has just purchased a quarter of the most delightful lemon haze but he is unable to skin up himself. What I want you to do is take him home, you’ve got the car right ?” The lads nodded. ”Well what I would like you to do is take Graham home, quick polite chat with Mrs Gee if you please.” Graham laughed. ”Then stay for the twenty minutes or half an hour it takes you two to roll the whole baggie into spliffs, place them all in a sealable container, say a polite good–bye to Mrs Gee, and head back here, capiche ?”

“Capiche.” The lads answered in unison.

“Oh you’re a saint sir you truly are,” Graham praised.

"No worries !" Beamed The Man.

"Give you a hand if you like..?" Offered one of the lads to Graham. "Oh thank you" he replied and offered his cane to the other lad, and slowly and considerately the three of them made their way out of the shop.

Jim looked at The Man, "we can't offer every customer that service you know."

The Man looked at Jim, "one starfish" he replied.

The next customers were a pair, siblings, the boys made the assumption the elder one was there at the behest of the younger one.

The older one nodded a hello and mumbled, 'so you can buy dope here ?'

"Yes if you're over twenty-one" The Man responded.

"I am" responded the older one presenting a driving license.

"Then what would you like ?"

"Acapulco Gold" snapped back the younger sibling.

The Man kept his eyes on the older sibling, "what would you like ?"

"Acapulco Gold" dutifully repeated the older sibling.

"Coming up." Stated The Man.

Whilst the siblings were being served more and more customers began to enter the shop, excited anticipation began to permeate the air, Jim slipped from behind the counter and encouraged the customers to form a line, Rob began working the till like an automaton, as customers gathered at the door The Man greeted them, swiftly explained there was a queue in the shop and hastily arranged a queue along the pavement, on the safe side of the bollards.

Less than two hours had passed before the queue ran past the shops and out on to the main road. The Man's security detail turned up, two males each around six foot four tall, both dressed all in black, The Man showed them where the head of the queue was and pointed out where it stretched to and with that the two men took up positions either end of the queue, all was calm.

The Man re-entered the shop and he, Jim and Rob worked the store, "please decide quickly" became their most frequently uttered phrase. The CLA registration machine confirmed their hundredth customer within two hours, and had chimed up three hundred in three hours. For a brief moment Jim, Rob, and The Man were united behind the counter, they shared an intensely satisfying smile. "Gentlemen, clink" spoke Jim. "Clink" grinned Rob, "Clink indeed" smiled The Man.

Around four pm The Man asked his security detail to prevent anyone else from joining the queue. Over the ensuing hour the atmosphere in the shop morphed from excitement to relief as the final few customers took their turns to be served. As the final purchaser was ushered from the shop, The Man thanked and tipped his security detail, the door was shut and the display lights turned off. The Man, Jim and Rob sank to their knees and laughed. The sheer relief of not having to do anything flooded through them. Rob looked up trying to stop laughing, but saw Jim descending into fits of giggles while The Man the man shook his head from side to side sniggering. Jim began to pant, desperately drawing in oxygen to suppress his guffaws. Twas The Man who regained the ability to speak first.

"How many ?"

Rob laughed.

"Go on, how many ?"

"One thousand two hundred and forty-six."

Dropped jaws and raised eyebrows from Jim and The Man.

"One thousand two hundred and…" Mouthed Jim "That's a darn few more than we ever got in the jewellers."

"That's a damn many more than could ever fit on the park bench" echoed The Man.

"Next ?"

"Same again tomorrow, for our sakes let's keep it to nine to five, the same company that provided the lads today will be doing frequent drive-bys tonight, the back door is bolted and the adjoining door locked, gentlemen we exit from the front, roller shutters down, we all head to our homes and see you here tomorrow." Jim and Rob did as The Man suggested and having secured down the metal shutters with two separate padlocks, Jim pocketed the keys, they fist bumped and parted ways, except Rob who turned back to Jim, "Pub ?"

"Pub."

Jim and Rob took their seats in the pub, clinked glasses and agreed it had been a good day. Each gulped their pints with such appreciation that a second was required within four minutes. The second pint too was well appreciated, though slower. Rob took his half-drunk second pint, tilted it away from himself and admired it. "That is good," he said, following on, "Hey let's do it, let's have the alcohol versus marijuana debate. "

"Well it's two different things ain't it, alcohol gets you up there ," Jim mimed being a football fan, "and marijuana gets you out there," Jim mimed taking a long toke and staring off into space.

"Aah well I reckon that what you is saying," responded Rob, "is that alcohol is a social thing, while marijuana is a private thing, and I'm saying well yes but that only applied up until ten o'clock this morning, situation gonna change."

"Yep." Agreed Jim. "But they do remain two different types of intoxicants, alcohol is dutch courage, dope is….low down confusion."

Rob nodded.

"And given that equation" continued Jim, "I want to ask which of the two intoxicants, when used to excess, causes the most societal problems ?"

"Alcohol."

Clink.

"So maybe" said Jim "what we have started doing today is easing and soothing society's problems."

"Well we ain't saints yet.." countered Rob," what we are is drug dealers, legal drug dealers."

"And how do you feel about yourself ?" Asked Jim.

"Fucking great !"

Clink.

IV. The Meal

When The Man, Jim and Rob arrived at the store for eight thirty the following morning the queue had already started to form. "We will not be opening until nine, you will all be served." The Man informed them and he, Jim and Rob slipped around to the backdoor of the shop, Jim had a large package under his arm, so Rob and The Man took the keys from him and started tackling the various locks, once inside and into the backroom Jim tore open the package to reveal a selection of brown overcoats. "Gentlemen" Jim announced "We have our uniform." Rob selected his size and length put on the coat and dove his hands into the pockets for a satisfying rummage, Jim selected his size, slipped on the garment, buttoned it up and proudly tapped an imaginary badge on the breast pocket. The Man selected his coat, threw it onto his shoulders and allowed its' sleeves to accept his arms, he first buttoned it right to the top, but after due consideration undid the top button and topped off the look with sunglasses. Jim and Rob applauded.

From nine am the shop was flooded with people. Those that were not purchasing perused the display stand of bongs, papers and novelty lighters. All the customers had been queuing outside together for an hour or more and a certain sense of community had evolved, the boys started to try and impress the girls with their knowledge of arabic gum and acacia trees, a few customers tried to demonstrate the best angle for a bong to be held at, while many other could not but help imitate skinning up in anticipation as they awaited their turn to be served.

Throughout the day the scanner kept registering customers, the till kept beeping and the drawers kept releasing their sacred contents. Each customers' anxious anticipation was soon replaced by grinning possession of the little green herb. Legal Jims soon chalked up its' two thousandth customer and was swiftly heading towards three thousand as five pm approached. Rob watched the little green light on the customer registration machine flick off and on whilst not that many miles the female engineer was seated in the basement of the CLA building watching a similar green light lighten and darken at an identical rhythm. She plugged a wire into the socket beneath the light and Legal Jim's customer list appeared on her laptop screen which she tilted to show her boss, the official who had conducted the interview with Jim a few weeks previously.

The engineer spoke, "There we go we have a full, and updating, record of every customer of Legal Jims. The system does also record the details of all those who provided id but were then refused, we don't have the details of those who the staff turned down prior to reference to the machine, but we'd really need video from inside the shop for that ?"

"Do we have that ?" Asked the boss.

"Not currently."

"Is it an option ?"

"If we insisted on cameras being installed and we installed them ourselves we could certainly build something in."

"Excellent, please bear that in mind. Our elected lords and masters are very keen on examining every little aspect of this little social experiment, and the numbers and the reactions of Legal Jim customers being turned away could become a very pertinent piece of the picture. In the meantime thank you, please do keep monitoring, do let me know if any celebrities or royalty crop up and I will keep the MP informed of all the good work we are doing.

The engineer and the manager smiled at each other.

At five pm on the third day the staff of Legal Jims once more sunk to the floor in sheer exhausted relief. They were still laughing, but they were tired from it.

"We'll have the returning customers starting from tomorrow, I'll arrange re-up over this evening and tomorrow," noted The Man.

"We need more staff," stated Rob.

"Agreed" said Jim "and I'm thinking we could ask the CLA for another machine."

"Sounds like a plan," concurred The Man.

"Right" said Rob, " I've got somewhere to be, got to tell a couple of guys I won't be working for them no more, til the morning." "Til the morning" replied Jim and The Man as Rob left. "I'm gonna stay and make a few calls," said the Man, "and I'll head home and send that e-mail" followed on Jim. Twenty minutes on the tram brought Jim to within walking distance of home, and he was soon satisfyingly closing the flat's front door, with him on the inside. In the living room Steve was slumped in a chair, Imogen was embedded in the sofa while a sorceress conjured up a spell on the telly. Jim slumped into the available chair with a smile. Steve paused the sorceress mid spell and looked across, "So how's the upgrade going ?"

"Nearly five thousand customers in the first three days."

"Fuck me there sure are a lot of fuckwits in Croydon."

"Bless 'em all each and everyone."

Steve breathed in haughtily.

"What is it your selling ?" Asked Imogen.

"You know" interjected Steve.

"I know I know I just want Uncle Jim to tell me, or would that be breaking the law ?"

Jim remained silent.

"Come on now Uncle it's all round school, everyone's hitting on their big brother or sisters to go buy some now that it's legal."

"It's not legal," replied Jim, "and there's good reason for that," he continued unconvincingly, "it's just that I have paid for a licence."

"So if you have a licence it's legal when someone's with you ?"

"No. it's the premises that have the licence."

"So it's legal to smoke in your shop ? "

"No. Absolutely not. It is legal to dispense from my shop and consume off the premises, you know like an off licence."

"So any sound person over twenty-one can come into your shop buy grass ?"

"Yes but they don't have to." Steve firmly interjected.

"And your Father is absolutely and entirely right with those words" concurred Jim rising from the sofa and leaving the room with his head bowed.

Once within his room Jim firmly laid a draft excluder across the base of the door, pulled a little 'erb from work from his pocket, grinding it, and sensitively mixing it with some tobacco on a piece of gummed paper resting on his desk he took the requisite construction and swivelled into a perfect gentling expanding cone topped off with the neatest of knots. Mmm.. Jim smiled, he took his creation to the window, leant out as far as he safely could and lit the tip of his torch. He inhaled and smiled. There was a bit of him that wanted to review and problem solve in advance what might be coming next, but there was also a big part of him that wanted to dwell on the smiles and happy moments of the past few days, that was the part of himself he went with.

Jim slept well. He awoke and was at work for half eight, as were The Man and Rob, swiftly joined by Matthew and Simon, the big fuckers. A management meeting was held in the car park at the back of the shop, and it was decided Maui Waui was best for a morning smoke. With that settled the men took their positions at the door, till and drawers, and The Man opened the shop. Day four of retail activity continued with what had become standard for the shop, customers pouring in with a sense of awe and wonder, eyes widened, nostrils narrowed as those who entered inhaled the wondrous combined aromas that filled the air at Legal Jims. People filed in, the five thousandth customer was registered around midday and by the close of play the sixth thousandth six hundred and sixty-sixth customer had been recorded. After the shutters went down a further staff meeting was held in the car park hosted by Hindu Kush. It was ten, maybe fifteen minutes into the meeting when someone first spoke. It was The Man. "Is everybody happy ?" He asked. Everyone contemplated, and slowly everyone nodded. The Man nodded in response to their nodding, he continued, "and is there anything anybody needs ?.." Jim and Rob shook their heads, Matthew shook his head, Simon didn't, he raised his hand, The Man raised his eyebrows and Simon spoke falteringly, "well it isn't a need as such it's just there's this girl see…" The Man, Jim and Rob looked at Simon, Matthew didn't seemingly already aware of the girl's existence. Simon continued, "Well this shop is famous right, and she would be so impressed if she could turn up here, and I could like, nod her in."

"So she would be turning up with a group of friends who get to see her being nodded in, and they in turn would be expecting to be nodded in too ?" Questioned The Man.

"Oh no" responded Simon, "she doesn't have any friends", Matthew concurred, Simon continued, "it's just that the feeling she would get from walking past all those people and straight to the head of the queue, well.."

"Well that would directly benefit you" The Man completed the sentence. "Just one person…" he breathed requesting confirmation, "just one person" declared Simon. "We can do that" stated The Man. Grunts were exchanged and Simon, Matthew and The Man left the meeting. "I am getting an uber from this very spot" declared Rob and started pressing the necessary parts of his mobile screen, "Wanna piggie ?" "Tram does it for me, " Jim responded ", I know it's still public transport but its' speed lifts the mood. "Important to get home happy," nodded Rob. The tram did indeed whisk Jim home in perfunctory time, and once more Steve and Imogen where viewing a sorceress on the TV, only this time her eyes were black. Jim and Steve locked eyes for a moment and Jim retired immediately to his room, once within his attention turned to the computer and specifically the e-mail reply from the CLA.

Dear Mr Pemberton,

With respect to your request for a second registration machine we are able to supply what you require however the cost of these machines in in excess of £50000. If we were to supply a second machine we must insist that they are kept under video surveillance. It would be remiss if these machines were stolen and we had not taken this basic step to protect them. Please let us know how you wish to proceed

The Cannabis Licencing Authority.

Despite the warning questioning the necessity of printing e-mail that followed Jim went ahead and printed. He folded the print out and slipped it into the pocket of his brown overcoat, then took off and hung up the coat. He lacked the energy to take off the rest of his clothes, his shoes, or even skin-up, Jim simply collapsed into sleep. Day five of retail began spritely. Maui Waui hosted the morning pow wow, there was some grinning, some shrugging, a little muffled laughing, but still nothing was really spoken until ten minutes in when The Man fired Simon a questioning look. "Around ten o'clock" replied Simon tentatively. The Man nodded. This interchange sparked Jim's Brain into life, he thrust his hand into his pocket pulling out and holding-up the print-out.

"You have in your hand a piece of paper…" questioned The Man.

"Yes that does not guarantee peace in our time. The CLA say if they give us a second machine its' gotta come with video cameras."

"They want to keep an eye on us, see what's going on.."

"Uh huh"

"Cameras at the front are okay…"said Rob, toking.

"We would need to be in control of them." Stated The Man.

"I'll reply," noted Jim. The men went to work.

Friday unfolded in many similar ways as had Monday to Thursday, only with more singing and dancing from the customers. Poses of anticipation awe and excitement were broadcast across a variety of platforms, eager hushed words were spoken prior to purchase, gushings of glee were espoused afterwards. At about twenty past ten Simon popped his head in the door and caught The Man's eye. The Man nodded. Simon ushered his girl in. She was tall, she was elegant, swept back long luscious deep brown hair, eyes concealed by the slightly tinted sunglasses resting on her delicate nose. She didn't so much walk past the queueing throng as glide, Simon followed in her wake, Matthew remained in position at the door shaking his head mournfully. She arrived at the counter and Simon took his place at her side. The young man at the head of queue glazed over at the sight of Simon's girl and acquiesced his position as quickly as he could. Jim was serving, he looked at the girl, looked away and awaited a request, she smiled, she lowered her sunglasses and looked to Simon. Gently he took her handbag from her shoulder and pulling out her purse handed the identification to Jim. Next he gently took her finger, she giggled, then he manipulated it on to the bed of the scanner, the blue lights shone over both digit and ID, Jim nodded his confirmation of the customer registration and handed the ID back to Simon.

" What'll it be ? "

"She'd like Hindu Kush" replied Simon.

"Coming right up" replied Jim with a smile.

The girl smiled, Simon smiled that she smiled, the young man at the head of the queue smiled because they were smiling. Jim flipped shut the bag and slid it beneath the stamp in a slick and practiced manoeuvre, presenting the pack before the girl with his lower hand whilst removing his top hand in a flamboyant reveal. She giggled, Simon's smile continued, he then reached across and took the pack from Jim and placed it in her purse, the girl in turn smiled her smile, turned beautifully on her heel, and walked demurely from the shop, Matthew held the door open as she glided out into the street, Simon patted his thanks to Matthew's elbow and swiftly followed. She and Simon stood there silently momentarily, then the girl raised her hand to his cheek and brushed her palm gently downwards, then leant forward and lightly kissed the area she'd just brushed.

"Thank you Darling" she whispered, then despite the presence of the bollards, she once more completed a most elegant turn and strode off towards the town centre, she did not look back.

The working day continued apace, as Matthew closed the door on the last customer Rob declared they had just recorded their eight thousand nine hundred and twenty third customer. The Man smiled satisfactorily, Jim let out a 'phewee' and Simon nodded his approval, The Man looked up at Simon and questioned "you gone ?" "I'm gone" replied Simon and he was, Matthew bolted the door behind him.

"We're here tomorrow and Sunday ?" questioned The Man.

"The customers are certainly expecting it" retorted Jim.

"We should start drawing wages" added Rob.

"When would you spend it ?" queried Jim.

The Man pointed to the sky. "Give me tomorrow." He declared. "Give me tomorrow, to go and round up a few faces conduct a few interviews and I will be here Sunday, maybe with a new assistant, certainly with news." Jim and Rob nodded their ascent, Matthew unbolted the door and The Man strode from the shop.

Left together Rob asked of Jim "that wages thing does need sorting out"

"You're absolutely right mate, shit we haven't even agreed an hourly rate, we should, and please do give me time to do the accounts properly, but in the meantime, need any cash ?"

"A couple of hundred would help."

Simon reached into his wallet and took out three hundred and swiftly handed it to Rob.

"Cheers mate" acknowledged Rob.

The two patted each other's shoulders and Rob left the shop.

"I've locked and bolted the back door" confirmed Matthew, "Come on let's do the shutters" he muttered leading Jim from the shop. Jim locked the door from the outside stood back and Matthew pulled down the shutters and knelt down to padlock them to the ground, at that moment a voice behind them spoke.

"Oi Mister"

Jim spun around, Matthew raised up slowly.

"You that cunt that's selling dope legally ?"

Jim looked at his interlocutor but his face was concealed by a bandana and beanie hat, three or four young men stood behind him, their faces similarly covered. Matthew clenched his fists. Jim turned slightly to totally confirm the presence of Matthew by his side and having done so turned back and stated assertively.

"Yes I am that cunt."

"Well you're putting us out of business you wanker ! I represent the association of street dealers and these are our streets, these were our customers and this is our livelihood and you you bastard are taking it from us !"

"Wait.. wait.. the association of street dealers ? You guys have a union !?"

"We function as a loosely held together co-operative, a co-operative that you are putting out of business !"

"Well I think that's the point ! I only sell to responsible over twenty-ones, surely you've still got the kids and the nu…, the mentally afflicted to sell to, which you really shouldn't you know."

"Says you ?" The you bounced off Jim's face, resounded into the shutters of his dope shop and echoed into the streets beyond.

"Yes." Responded Jim "I follow rules."

"Hey we got a code, we don't target the kids, not the really young ones anyway, and a lot of the nutters consider it as medicine. But what you're doing is taking all the good business, the regular folks with ready cash, you are taking a bite out of the best bit of our pie."

The representative of the association of street dealers leant forward locking eyes with Jim, Matthew leant forward and growled gently.

“I think the world is changing” stated Jim softly “and that you need to find a new pie.”

“Our streets” stated the rep and leaned back from Jim and indicated that the boys behind him should disperse.

The rep raised his index finger towards Jim, “You’ve been warned”

“Yes, yes I have” confirmed Jim nodding his confirmation, the rep nodded in acknowledgement and set to leave “By the way” interrupted Jim, “If you’re ever looking for a job where you do what you’re doing now, but responsibly, you know where to find me.” The rep looked at Jim and nodded, then melted away into the night.

Jim and Matthew looked at each other, Jim shrugged, Matthew smirked, “hey” he piped up, “these are his streets you know, want company to the tram stop ?” “Can’t be too careful, ”said Jim smiling his thanks, “so tell me about Simon’s girl, stunning or what !?” “Oh yes” sighed Matthew, “But high maintenance, very high maintenance.” “She did look it.” Concurred Jim.

Deep within the bowels of the CLA manager, the female engineer who had installed the equipment, and her male counterpart were reviewing the information.

“Eight-thousand nine hundred and twenty-three customers,” stated the manager, ”they’ve had a good first week.”

“We don’t know what their expenses are ?” Countered the male.

“That we don’t,” concurred the lady, ”but we do know that they have received four hundred and seventy-six thousand nine hundred and twenty pounds this week.”

“From the eight thousand nine hundred and twenty-three original purchases plus three thousand two hundred and seven customers making return purchases. Yes.” Stated the engineer.

“Of those customers how many have been turned away due their names appearing on other databases ?”

“Zero.”

“Zero ?”

“I saw pictures of the shop of the news,” interjected the male, “they had a couple of large men stationed by the door, and there were considerable queues, maybe this put off.. those who are not eligible.”

“I expect so” sighed the manageress, “it would be nice to have a test case to know the system worked. There has been a lot of media interest in the shop and all aspects must be scrutinized, I would like to establish the video feed as soon as possible so we are the first to know what goes on in this budding little business.”

The male smiled slightly, the engineer did not.

Jim was stoned. He was mightily stoned. He lay on the floor of his room arse against the wall, legs pointed upwards and knees hooked over the window sill his sockless feet wiggling in the night air. He was giggling, he was laughing from within his very core. He didn’t have to look for a happy thought to find, the last week had brought so many. Here he was managing England’s first legal dope shop ever ! The customers were exuberant, the profits staggering, the competition was scared and he Jim Pemberton was, quite possibly for the first time in his life, in the right place at the right time, Jim smiled himself to sleep. Then it started to rain and he was awoken by the quivering of his own toes.

Saturday at Legal Jims had begun before Jim, Rob, Matthew and Simon arrived. The queue already stretched for fifty metres prior to nine o’clock, it was a polite and organised queue, but most insistent, though despite the absence of The Man the morning meeting took place as unscheduled as ever. Once the smoking was done and the butts stubbed and concealed the men prepared for work, Jim felt a need to speak, which he did, “Guys today will be hard… but tomorrow will be better.” Matthew and Simon nodded, Rob muttered “aye.”

Eight thousand nine hundred and twenty-three had become well in excess of twelve thousand by the time Matthew and Simon ushered the last customer out the door at five pm. Working nine to five constantly on their feet, with only a few swift tense pee breaks, was taking its' toll on the staff. As Matthew and Simon attended to the shutters and doors, Rob closed up the drawers and till, Jim took the opportunity to swiftly speak up, "Guys, bloody well done on today, and on everyday so far, tomorrow will be easier, The Man will return tomorrow with.. whatever news he brings, if we agree to cameras we'll have a second till up and running in no time, so just saying I know it's a strain and well thank you for coping."

"No worries Jim," replied Simon, "yeah it's longer hours than we're used to, but the customers are easier to deal with than the night club crowd."

"And me mum saw me face on the telly the other night," piped up Matthew, "she thinks I'm standing here trying to stop people coming into the shop, so it's all good."

Jim and Rob sniggered. Jim laughed further and then held up a sign to which the others all concurred, it read, 'It is Sunday Morning. We will be opening at ten o'clock." Jim secured the sign in a cellophane wallet and Rob taped it to the outside of the shutters whilst Matthew and Simon scanned the shadows for interlopers, though the staff of Legal Jims remained unaccosted that night and the gentlemen nodded to each other and made their separate ways home.

Sunday morning, it was a shame to get up and have to go to work, oh but what work, safely supplying pleasure to thousands. There was balance in Jim's mind. Right place, right time, right people. Negative events will occur, that is the truth of existence, but the robust positives in place will continue to carry Legal Jims to great heights, and great profitability, Jim smiled and this was followed by his brain reporting back to him that it was well okay for him to smile. He had taken the risks and he was earning the rewards, the smile was fully authorised.

Jim turned down the spliff at the morning meeting. The Man shot him a questioning look, he beamed back beatific contentment in return. Rob hurriedly took Jim's designated tokes in addition to his own and passed it on to Simon, he toked, Matthew also passed.

"So" announced The Man, "We are in agreement that we are in acceptance of a second machine with cameras.." General nodding. "And when you make that communication with the powers that be.."

"The C L A…" intoned Jim dramatically.

"Well I have a question for the C L A", mimicked The Man, "we know and we agree our customers must be over twenty-one, what about the staff ?"

Eyebrows raised.

"The two lads from the first day who helped out the old man, I trust them both implicitly, but neither is yet twenty-one."

Rob spoke up, "I mean I ain't a dad of anything like that yet, but is working in a dope shop really the right job for any young lad ?"

"After what they've seen growing up around here," retorted The Man, "ain't no big thing."

Rob nodded his understanding.

"You know the CLA have checked me out to the nth degree, they've checked out my family, my home, the premises, the business, but not once have they inquired about or set rules about the staff that I employ. I see no reason to bring that oversight to their attention." Jim looked at the man, "You say they're honest and hard-working, you vouch for them ?"

The Man nodded.

"Well what size coats do they need ?"

The Man smiled and the five men cheerfully stood and made their way to work, The Man slapped Simon on the back saying, "And hey was your girl impressed with our set-up and service the other day ?"

"Damn straight !" Replied Simon eagerly, "first her face was on the telly, then her face was on my.."

The Man slapped Simon again and the men went to work.

The quietness of Sunday morning pervaded the shop, the customers shared the muted tone, even those livestreaming from the queue restrained their vocality in respect to the time of the week. Each customer approached the counter timidly, then swiftly relished the opportunity to speak the name of their intended purchase, out loud and with pride, and whether it was Jim, The Man or Rob at the counter the server would always reply with an approving mischievous grin in return. It happened to be Jim at the counter when a young lady with sunglasses resting upon her nose peering over the top of the lenses approached the counter.

Jim raised his eyebrows questioningly.

"Ooh I'm happy to let you decide," was the lady's opening line. "And if I were after a little more than a little hashish to whom should I speak ?" The lady reached for her glasses and lowered down her nose.

"Why.." Smiled Jim " Whatever do you mean ?"

"Oh my interest, at this stage, is completely professional. This is the hottest shop in town, I work for the newspaper and we would love to do an interview."

"Oh my apologies," replied Jim, "we don't do advertising."

"Oh this would be an interview, not an advert"

"Don't they essentially amount to the same thing ?"

The lady dropped her gaze and changed tac. "Is it because you've been told not to advertise ?"

"We choose not to advertise."

"Because you don't need to ?"

"Ethics."

"On account of you sell intoxicants ?"

"I thought you were here to purchase intoxicants ?"

"I am. What do you recommend ?"

"Northern Lights. A good entry level smoke, I'll prepare you a quarter, and if I may request proof of ID and a scan of your finger please."

The lady journalist smiled acknowledgingly and lowered her gaze to her handbag whilst speaking, "You know my paper will run a story on this shop regardless of your ethics. If you agree to have dinner with me tonight that will at least give you the chance to have me hear your view on events, no pictures, no tagging, and it being a story the bill goes on the company account, so it's on me, whaddya say ?"

Jim sealed the lady's quarter of Northern Lights and handed it back to her along with her identification, she took hold of the items before he let go and took a firm grip on his gaze, "The story is the story either way. I'm giving you the chance to have an input into that, and besides dinner with me isn't that bad a way to spend an evening. The journalist took her sunglasses from her nose and scrunched it appealingly.

"Okay"

"Brilliant ! Meet you here after you shut ?"

"Okay"

She swirled and sashayed from the shop.

Jim tried to look away, felt like he shouldn't, then felt like he really should so did, then looked back.

The day proceeded, towards the end of the seventh day of trading of Legal Jims the fifteenth thousand customer was recorded. A little after four an awkward gangly white youth approached the counter, as Jim attempted to assess his age the youth began speaking in a hesitant manner, "I am sorry about the other night, calling you a cunt and that, soz I was out of order, and you know if you're serious about that job I know my stuff and can serve customers quickly.."

“Are you old enough to shop here ?”

“Twenty-three as it happens.”

“Got proof ?”

The twenty three year old passed Jim a driving licence. Jim studied the photo, its’ appearance and the person standing before him matched.

“So Paul Thompson, what will you select ?”

“Well Sativa strains have the reputation for being more up-lifting and like, giving a more cerebral head-high whereas Indica are more recommended for relieving pain and insomnia, and well seeing as I feel fine right now and simply feel like getting high please sir may I have a quarter of Bubba Kush.”

Jim smiled as he prepped the order. He nodded to Paul, Paul acknowledged his nod.

“And can you be here at eight thirty tomorrow morning ?”

“I can.”

“See you then.”

Paul bowed and left the shop quietly. Rob took over the till. The Man sidled up to Jim. “Okay with him and my two that’s three new staff members from the morning, you tell the CLA yes to a new machine and we are rolling at twice the speed my man, I shall be arranging the re-ups, and I hear that you are out with a journalist tonight ?...”

“I don’t think I got the chance to say no.”

“Hah ! Enjoy my man, we’ve always said you are the face of the operation, go out there and show it.”

Jim laughed.

“Hey at the worst it’s free food, have fun now I am out of here ! Jim, Rob, Matthew, Simon, I will see you in the morning.” The Man swung open the front door intending to sweep from the shop however he found the doorway blocked by the lady journalist. She quickly appraised the situation, smiled politely and stepped into the shop and to the side, The Man completed his sweeping exit. Jim could see the questions forming on the journalist’s face, he handed his brown jacket and the keys to Rob with a “see you in the morning” and hurried over to where the journalist was standing.

“Hello again…” began Jim.

“Kathryn. It’s Kathryn,” Kathryn said shaking hands.

“And I’m Jim” replied Jim.

“As in the Jim of Legal Jim fame ?”

“Well I suppose so yes, we wanted to call it legal symbol, but you can’t have symbol on legal documents.”

“So the first legal dope shop in the UK became Legal Jims..”

“First legal cannabis shop for hundred and ten odd years. The Brits of course did used to forcibly sell the stuff internationally, the opium war ‘n all that..”

“Oh yes, I’ve heard of that, weren’t there a couple of sequels too ?”

Jim laughed.

Kathryn continued, “and so you’re continuing that war ?..”

Jim thought for a moment.

“War is over.” He tentatively declared, spreading his hands outward to show the shop’s wares.

As Kathryn looked around Jim continued, “There’s been pubs in this country for thousands of years, and there were certainly opium dens in the past…though please do look around, this shop is no den, no under twenty ones and we do not serve to people who are not in a fit state to consume our products. This shop is the evolution of society’s relationship with marry ju ana, not a revolution. Because you know what, in this life, it is okay to have a drink and a schmoke and I am happy, even possibly, almost a little bit proud of making that happen.”

Matthew, Simon and Rob who had been watching from the counter broke out in mock applause.

Kathryn acknowledged the audience. Stared each man in the face and asked to the room “Does smoking cause cancer ? “

Jim said nothing. Rob spoke up, “Yes, yes it does.” Matthew and Simon nodded their agreement.

“And does your shop encourage smokers ?”

Matthew and Simon looked at each other, Rob looked at his feet, Jim spoke up, " it caters for existing smokers. And there are far worse vices in this life than smoking and far more things such as knives guns bombs and missiles that will kill you a lot quicker than a spliff, indeed if more people were to reach for spliffs rather than weapons what a wonderful world this would be."

Jim sang the end of his speech to more mock applause from the audience and he mock bowed his appreciation.

"Nicely put Jim," said Kathryn, "buy you supper ?"

Jim smiled his agreement, nodded to Rob, Matthew and Simon, and followed Kathryn out of the door.

Out on the street Kathryn spoke, "I pre-googled local restaurants looking for somewhere quiet, there's a Lebanese/Mediterranean place ten minutes' walk from here noted for its' calm ambience"

"Lead the way"

As they walked they talked.

"So you've been open for one week, you literally have queues of customers going round the block, any backlash as yet ?"

"We've not had anyone picketing us if that's what you mean."

"And no attempted break-ins ?"

"Not so far, we have constant security while we're open and a private security firm patrols the rest of the time, I know we're a target, I think we're as prepared as possible."

"There's been quite a reaction on line."

"I've been pretty busy with work, 'fraid I've missed it."

"The kids are very excited that dope can now be bought legally."

"The kids cannot buy it legally."

"That's why they're excited."

Jim laughed again, “I think they are put off by the security, and the grown up nature of the queues, they haven’t been trying, which I think is what decriminalization is about.”

“Decriminalization, that’s the word you use.”

“I do not know the proper legal term. Cannabis remains illegal under the misuse of drugs act, my store is legally permitted to sell cannabis, the law is in a state of flux. When I use the word decriminalization I mean in the mind of the smoker, getting yourself high is not a sinful act, it is a lot more beautiful than a lot of other activities, it’s okay to do it.”

“And can swiftly lead to mental health problems, smoking related problems and a dependency on intoxicants.”

“Is that where you really stand, on the side of the negative waves ?”

“Hey I’m just after the story, I don’t have an opinion, just the facts sir.”

Jim laughed at the imitation serious intonation. They reached the restaurant and through glances established it to be low key and convivial as reviewed, a staff member welcomed them with a wide smile and a few words and led Jim and Kathryn to a secluded table, after handing them the menus they asked, “would you like drinks ?”

Jim looked questioningly at Kathryn, “do you drink red ?” she retorted, Jim nodded, “please” continued Kathryn to the waiter, “may we have a bottle of your best red.”

“That would be a Rioja Crianza at..”

“It doesn’t matter, that will be fine.”

The waiter exited smiling.

“Have you eaten Lebanese/Mediterranean before ?” asked Kathryn ?

“Not that I can recall.”

“Me neither.”

Kathryn scanned the menu, “Fattoush followed by Shish Taouk,” looks good she stated.

“I’ll have the same.”

“Right” began Kathryn folding her arms, “The story so far is a dope shop named Legal Jims has opened up in Croydon.”

“Out of curiosity” interjected Jim, ”what word are you going to use, not dope surely, cannabis or marijuana ?”

“What word do you use ?”

“Either work, I always prefer marijuana, more sing song”

“Editor’s decision,” muttered Kathryn, “So a legitimate marijuana shop has opened in Croydon, there’s queues round the block, what’s next on the agenda ?”

“Well our first order of business has been to arrange a new till,” smiled Jim, “they are not just regular tills, they contain the security system that verifies the customer’s age and identity, so once that’s in place I do hope we can speed up service and reduce the inconvenience to Croydonites of there being queues on the street.” Smiled Jim sweetly.

“So every customer has a background check done of them ?”

“Err no, the checks confirm age and identity and well to be honest I don’t know what other databases it checks against, something medical I think, people with a medical history of a bad reaction to marijuana..”

“Is there a database for that ?”

Jim shrugged.

“So although you’re government licenced marijuana possession remains illegal, and the growing of plants remains illegal, where does your stock come from ?”

Jim smiled.

“Do you believe you can keep up with demand ?”

Jim held up crossed fingers.

“Do you think the government licensing the legal selling of marijuana encourages drug taking ?”

Jim thought for a while, Kathryn looked at him demandingly requesting at least some sort of reply to one of her questions.

Jim spoke, “The government didn’t issue my license, the cannabis licensing authority did.”

Kathryn acknowledged the answer.

Jim used her silence to initiate his own line of conversation, “In Arabic culture crowding round the hookah pipe is a normal social activity, I do agree a lot of smoking is bad for the brain, a little smoking is natural and nice, and well, quite beneficial, that’s the concept I’d like to introduce to the UK, there doesn’t have to be a conflict over the topic, especially where the issue is really like about avoiding conflict.”

“Hippy”

Jim laughed, thought, laughed again, and reviewed the review.

“Professional hippy.” He replied.

Kathryn nodded in recognition of his assessment. “So” she continued, “that ethos has led you to opening the UK’s first and so far only marijuana retailing establishment..”

“First legal establishment. I rather think that people have been selling the stuff before I came along,” Jim tapped his nose knowingly, Kathryn grinned, “First legal establishment,” she continued, ”and exploring that ‘legality’, marijuana remains officially illegal yet you have a licence to sell it, that surely is a situation that can’t continue , how do you see it progressing ?”

“Well yeah I agree you can’t proceed with conflicting laws, but listen hey marijuana exists and humans have employed it for millennia, people getting stoned and seeing strange things has been the start of many a religion, so I think dope does have that to apologise for, but beyond that it’s all good, inhaling de smoke it’s relaxing, uplifting, calming, soothing and inspiring, though yes however much marijuana is great for developed brains it is bad and is simply wrong for developing brains, no question. And this change that society is going through, taking marijuana distribution out of the hands of the drug dealers and into the hands of establishments like my own who do not sell to the under twenty-ones and do net sell to the incapacitated, is absolutely the right and proper direction in which to take society’s relationship with marijuana.”

“There are many doctors, medical professionals and people suffering from emphysema, bronchitis and COPD and parents who think smoking should be stubbed out.”

“You don’t have to smoke it, baking is an option.”

“As long as everybody must get stoned”

“That’s how the song goes.”

Kathryn looked up questioningly, “Bob Dylan,” explained Jim.

The two plate of vibrant green fattoush salad arrived and Kathryn and Jim dove straight in, through shrugs and blinks they agreed to forego interaction as buoyed by their stimulating conversation they each found themselves with vigorous appetites and made short work of the starter.

Kathryn restarted the conversation. “How long do you think the situation can last, cannabis being illegal yet you having a licence to sell ?”

“That is certainly not my decision to make. What people want is the deciding factor then it’s up to the laws we make to catch up, they will in time.”

What if what people want is bad for them ?”

“They had a vote in the house of commons, they said it was okay.”

Kathryn remained silent.

“Somebody had to decide something” shrugged Jim.

“And you are now in an ideal position to profit.”

“Yes.” “And to sell the ethos.”

Kathryn’s eyebrows raised.

“That getting a little stoned now again is pretty beneficial to the human condition. Escaping the pressures, letting your mind wander, indulging in thought experiments, being relaxed, pursuing a state of happiness, it’s all good.”

"Well I want to say clearly I'm not convinced, you can do all that thinking without the smoke inhalation and without the danger to your mental health. However you have made your point clearly too and I shall report your point of view precisely as you've conveyed it. Now as I said no pics, no tagging, no putting you on the spot, but do you want to be credited as a source close to the organisation, an employee of Legal Jims..

"ooh I like source close to the organisation."

"Then that's how it shall be. So Jim before becoming a legal licensed drug dealer what did you used do ?

Before Jim could reply Kathryn followed up, "were you like an amateur drug dealer, practicing down the alleys ?"

Jim laughed.

"Though to be fair you don't look the type," conceded Kathryn.

"I ran a jewellers."

Kathryn's eyebrows raised.

"Shop manager, not owner," continued Jim, "ran it for many years, always been a smoker on the side, the setting up of the CLA was my chance to combine what I know how to do with what I like to do."

"How do the two trades compare ?"

"The economics are so different, with a jewellers there are a lot less sales, but when you get a good one it can set the business up for a whole year. It's about cultivating relationships with the wealthy so it's you they choose to return to when they are in the mood to buy. With selling marijuana it's fling open the doors and let the people roll in, I swear there really hasn't been a need to cultivate a desire, jewellery is about the rich, dope is about the people."

"And you're a man of the people ?.."

"Well 'm certainly not one of the rich."

“So..”

“A moment if I may..” interjected Jim, “You’ve asked me the questions and I’ve given you answers, my turn, did you have any other jobs before becoming a journalist ?”

“Not major ones, I worked in a pet shop as a teenager and had thoughts of being a vet..”

“But”

“Couldn’t face clearing up all the poo. Did English at university and the idea of being one of those pioneering female journalists engulfed me and I decided to bravely head on out there determined to shine the light of truth on to crimes and wrong-doings”

“Yet hear you are reporting on how the UK is slowly saying yes to drugs, in Croydon.”

Kathryn laughed.

“It is the biggest news story around” she continued, “so thank you for agreeing to the dinner.”

“You’re welcome,” replied Jim, ”and thank you for… asking me honest questions. And all I can say is I and about seven million other people in the country use marijuana regularly because we, well I, like it. It gets you high, it puts you into a pleasant state of mind, lets you go random.. BUT of course a person should not drive a car stoned, should not operate heavy machinery stoned, or ideally not try and do anything responsible at all, getting stoned is most pleasant as a private thing, you know like sex used to be.”

Kathryn laughed though swiftly continued, “well it is exactly that.”

Jim’s eyebrows raised.

“A stoned person should not do anything responsible.”

Jim kept his eyebrows raised.

“Well what good is that ? Another stoner laying about on the couch going whoa man, how’s that gonna change the world.”

“Well it won’t but hopefully they’ll be happy.”

"And that's the point is it, just to be happy, what about achieving things, righting wrongs ?"

"You know that sounds good too."

"Good I'm glad it does."

Kathryn's statement coincided with the arrival of the Shish Taouk. The skewered meat was bathed in lemon and garlic overwhelming the diners with an aroma of anticipation. The waiter once more backed away smiling. As Kathryn and Jim tried to hide their saliva from one another the unspoken agreement not to disturb the others' eating came into play and Jim and Kathryn tucked in. They both thoroughly enjoyed their food. As each chewed their last morsels conversation began to resume.

"Well we go to print Wednesday and the paper will be out on Thursday, it's going to be front page, the UK's first licenced cannabis/dope/marijuana shop has opened in Croydon, and there's queues around the block. As promised I will not say I have had supper with Jim of Legal Jim's but I will quote 'a source close to the organisation' as saying well basically 'peace man' (Kathryn made the V symbol with both hands) and yes that you adamantly don't sell to under twenty-ones or the incapacitated, the picture will be from outside the shop, any issue with the guys you've got outside the shop ?"

"No, they've already been seen on the telly"

"Excellent, well Jim, thank you once more.."

Kathryn looked to the waiter who approached most courteously and who having already read her eyes produced the bill and card machine, Kathryn cheerfully presented her company credit card and carefully placed the bill in her purse. They rose to leave. Jim stood quietly while Kathryn organised her bag and coat and the ever anticipating waiter held the door open at the perfect time for Kathryn and Jim to be able to glide through while easily and swiftly relaying their thanks and gratitude for the meal. Outside on the street Kathryn and Jim faced each in goodbye stance. "So paper out on Thursday," he noted, "I will be sure to buy a copy" "The story will contain nothing but the truth," replied Kathryn, "I assure you," and with that she scrunched her nose, swivelled on her back foot and walked off into the night leaving Jim held in his goodbye stance.

Sunday night public transport took its' time in delivering Jim home, he didn't mind, he gazed into space and reviewed the evenings' conversation. Kathryn's line about stoners never achieving anything loomed foremost in his mind, he wished he retorted with hey well sometimes they start businesses with half million pound turnovers in the first week you know, but it was too late for that now. Jim recalled the tone of the evening, the essential debate as to between whether marijuana was a good thing, or a bad thing. Jim had always felt that it had been good because he'd always had positive experiences. Some people understandably think marijuana is bad because they have had negative experiences. And now that Jim was out there front and centre publically selling the mary jane, did that mean he was now defined as good or bad ? I'm out there giving people a choice he thought and admittedly a choice that could have bad consequences. Jim found the thought really heavy and decided he need to get home and have a smoke.

V. Closure

It was Monday morning, Jim snapped into life. Washed, shaved and brown jacket on within five minutes and five minutes later he was on the platform. He felt noticed as he stood on the train, nobody said anything of course, Jim debated to himself as to whether the uniform of Legal Jim's had become that well known, then he had the revelation that his work outfit may well have absorbed the odours of his work place. For anyone looking Jim attempted a facial expression that expressed understanding, acknowledgement, a little sheepishness coupled with mild mischievousness whilst also silently trying to communicate the words, 'it's okay, I have a licence' , then he swiftly stared at the floor.

Chocoloupe hosted the morning meeting, Jim, Rob, The Man, Matthew, Simon, nodded to each other, whilst the three others waited to be nodded at. The Man spoke first, "this is Anthony, this is Zeke." Anthony and Zeke delivered their nods, all reciprocated. Jim spoke next, "this is Paul", Paul nodded, once more all present nodded back. Jim continued, "okay" Jim took a toke, "mm, right well I contacted back the CLA over the weekend agreeing to their conditions so they'll be a second till soon, until then it's about you three getting trained on the till, I'm assuming your familiar with the products ?" All three of the new employees smiled their confirmation. "So if Rob you would like to do the honours and outfit Anthony, Paul and Zeke with their brown jackets, customise them as you wish gentlemen, and show them the system." "With pleasure," replied Rob who having stubbed out the spliff threw open the rear door to Legal Jims and showed the young men inside. In their absence The Man, Jim, Matthew and Simon formed into a natural square facing one another, Matthew, Simon and The Man looking each other straight in the eye, Jim had a good view of The Man's clavicle. He saw The Man reach across it and into an inside pocket pulling out a perfectly rolled joint protected within a transparent cigar tube. The Man carefully tapped it out onto his hand, placed the cardboard end firmly between his teeth and lit the fuse theatrically from a stone coloured zippo lighter. He inhaled deeply. He paused. Matthew, Simon and Jim waited for the pause to end. The Man passed the reefer to Matthew, who also inhaled deeply coughing slightly on the exhale. When Matthew's cough was done The Man finished his pause and began to speak. "Supply should not be a problem…what it would be nice would be to have a clear picture of demand." Jim nodded comprehendingly, Simon said, "Uh huh" and Matthew was staring at the little birdies overhead. "Plants take time to grow" continued The Man.

Then he stopped. Simon nodded repetitiously digesting his words, "Yes, yes they do," he confirmed. Jim realised the spliff had been passed down to him, and had stayed with him, he swiftly handed it on to Simon, Simon took at and stared at it for a while, Jim replied to The Man, "Well we've had fifteen thousand customers and nearly twenty five thousand sales in the first seven days. There's a start, with two tills, fifty thousand sales a week ?" The Man nodded his understanding, he reached out and took the spliff from Simon's hands and relit it. The spliff fizzled, the smoke flowed and the man drunk it in smoothly. "I'm gonna need a bigger farm," he murmured.

Eventually the little birdies flew away and Matthew brought his attention back down to earth, he pointed at the back door of Legal Jims and muttered, "should we ?" The others slowly concurred and floated slowly one by one into the shop. Matthew gingerly opened the door to the area behind the counter, the shop was humming smoothly, Rob was working the till while Anthony and Paul were preparing the product. Zeke, the tallest of the new recruits, had taken up position amongst the customers on the far side of the counter and was gently and most charmingly martialling them into a queue formation. Matthew indicated that Jim should also peak through the gap in the door, which he did, and like a pair of contented parents at a child's bedtime they softly closed the door.

Simon, Matthew, Jim and The Man took seats as best they could in the storage area at the back of the shop. The Man began to make phone calls, his patois so dense that the rest of the men couldn't make out the topic of conversation, the word up featured frequently, 'up scale', 'up production', 'up those numbers.' Then Simon reached for his own phone, he flipped across a couple of screens until he found what he was looking for, prepped his face then pressed a button, after a few moments he smiled, "hello baby.." Jim's phone flicked into life next, a phone call from a withheld number, Jim calculated the odds of it being a useful call, ignored them and answered anyway, listening silently.

"Mr Pemberton ?"

"Uh huh"

"This is the CLA, good morning."

"Good morning"

"Yes in response to your request for a second customer registration machine, and the cameras to cover them, our engineer tells us we're good to go so I'm calling to arrange installation."

"Excellent, I mean if things are indeed good to go, well how about this evening, we close at five."

The caller from the CLA went on mute for a few moments and then returned with, "yes certainly our installation team can be there at five this evening."

"Ooh well thank you, thanks for that and we'll see them then."

"You're welcome, goodbye."

Jim turned off the phone with a satisfying double tap looking up he saw that The Man had his eyes skyward fully engrossed in conversation, Simon stared at his screen enraptured by what he saw, Matthew was alert and looked to him questioningly followed by a glance to the door to the shop. With his hands Jim indicated calmness and that he would take a look see, Matthew acknowledged with a scrunch of his nose.

Jim opened the door to the shop. The joint was jumping, the shop was filled with starry eyed customers gazing in wonder at Legal Jim's delights, some gazed in wonder at the draws behind the counter eagerly reading the inscribed names and hugging each other in delight upon recognition, others took the bongs and mimed taking a deep satisfying lung busting toke from the exotic devices whilst other customers nodded knowingly at only the most expensive rolling papers. Anthony professionally organised the queue within the shop, Zeke had taken up position by the door and placating and informing the customers gathering on the street. Rob and Paul now interchanged between the till and baggie preparation frictionlessly sliding passing each other in their tasks. Jim waited until Rob was stationary and took up position next to him, "Good news good news, new till tonight."

"Tonight.."

"The CLA installation team will be here at five."

"Good."

As Paul slid passed he gave Jim a questioningly look to which Jim replied with a warm pat upon his shoulder, Anthony and Zeke gave inquisitive glances Jim held up both hands in a double thumbs up meant for all to see, then sidling back across to the door, carefully avoiding Paul's trajectory, Jim stood for a moment with his back to the door gazing out upon the shop, and crossed his arms in a gesture of absolute satisfaction at what he saw. "I am not a bad man," he decided.

Deep within his introspective moment Jim completely failed to notice The Man opening the door behind him and fell backwards, The Man caught him. "Always here for you man, always here," he murmured as he propped Jim back upright. "Cheers man," responded Jim, "and I have news for you, the new till is scheduled for five o'clock today." "Excellent !" Responded The Man, he pulled the door shut and pulled Jim closer, "And my growers are all understanding of the need to upscale their operations, though they will need paying" "No problem," responded Jim, "all you have to do is give me your name and account number and I'll set it up." "Hey no need to bring me into this" breathed The Man smoothly, " I have six growers, regular people with regular lives, you can set up standing orders straight to them, and there's various others who get stock in from elsewhere and I'll pay them cash ad hocly as and when, hey maybe we can start some weekly specials." "I like that' grinned Jim, "this weeks' guest bud !" "The Man smiled, "right" he said, "I'm off to scout some arable land, laters." The Man and Jim patted each others' shoulders and The Man exited swiftly and silently from the rear of the shop.

The ample number of staff at Legal Jims ensured the store's eighth day of trading passed swiftly. Rob, Anthony, Paul and Zeke rotated smoothly around the shop while Matthew and Simon were able to alternately take up position managing the queue on the street. Jim felt another moment of satisfaction early in the afternoon as the number of recorded customers topped eighteen thousand, he still felt there was a certain coming of age associated with the number eighteen, and he was delighted to inform the final customer he ushered out the door at five that they were the eighteen thousandth eight hundred and eighty-eighth person to make a purchase. Matthew spotted the arrival of the CLA van and brought it to Jim's attention who thanked Anthony, Paul and Zeke heartily for their work and suggested they slip out the back door, Matthew and Simon exited from the front leaving Jim and Rob to greet the CLA engineer, this time accompanied by three non-descript men with multiple boxes, Jim and Rob indicated they should place their boxes on the counter which the men duly did so whilst the engineer spoke.

"We have one further customer registration machine and four cameras. One for each machine, one to cover the front door, one to cover the back door."

"Not the back door !" responded Jim and Rob in unison.

The engineer looked up.

Speaking hesitantly she said, "It is logical, a camera for each machine and a camera for each exit and entrance.

"Listen," said Jim, "the machines and front door are fine, if they try to get in through the back door that means getting through two security doors and then they'll arrive at our wall of merchandise first which of course would be there actual intended target, no cameras at the back."

The engineer didn't react. One of the men who carried in the boxes shrugged slightly, "makes our job easier," he mumbled. The engineer accepted the situation. "Okay" she said, "the machine bolted to the counter as before. A camera in each of the front corners covering the machines and one outside covering the front door."

"Agreed" said Jim and the non-descript men set to work.

Rob fired a questioningly at Jim, Jim nodded, the two men slapped palms and Rob left the shop, Jim once more found a quiet spot to be out of the way as the non-descript men set to work and the engineer fiddled with her cat six cables.

Following two hours of drilling, screwing, adjusting and re-adjusting the cameras the second customer registration were fully installed. The engineer presented paperwork with Jim which he signed eagerly, the engineer nodded to Jim, then she nodded to her non-descript men, and the employees of the CLA duly filed from the shop. Jim swiftly bolted the door behind them. He assessed the cameras, they were on a fixed mounting pointed directly at the tills, leaving blind spots by the door and in the far corners. Well being observed is a fact of life he noted to himself having crossed the shop floor he did feel fell a certain satisfaction in disappearing from the cameras view into the back of shop.

Jim checked the back door, first opening and scanning the morning meeting area, reassuring himself that the area remained unobserved, then he slammed shut the back door, bolted it shut, patting the bolts to be sure, Jim then passed through from the rear to the front of that shop, locked the door and patted that lock, crossed the observed area of the shop, unbolting the front door to let himself out and turning to lock it behind him, with a pat. As he reached up to pull down the shutter Jim suddenly found himself bathed in light, he stopped moving, he heard a voice shout, "Now before he shuts it !" A car engine roared into life behind the light, Jim turned in slow shocked horror towards the light. The light, which were the headlights of a BMW X5 raced directly at him, Jim dropped to his knees.

The car smashed into the bollards. Neither gave way. The forward momentum of the car and its' curved lower bumper forced it upwards and the front end was launched into the air towering over Jim like a raging beast until it came crashing down impaling itself upon two bollards held firmly three feet in the air with the wheels spinning menacingly. On his knees Jim sucked in his breaths. There was a shout. "Fuck." The car lights went out, the car door slammed and footsteps ran off into the night. Jim continued to breathe. The wheels had stopped spinning. Jim rose to his feet, then felt he wasn't quite ready for this. He leant heavily against the shop window and after a few restorative moments felt able to stand and turned to look the car right in the grill. Jim managed a smile, he reached out to the concrete beams that had protected both him and the shop and grasped them and held them, "Fucking great bollards" he breathed.

Jim was still clinging to the bollards when a man in a uniform turned up, the man stared in open mouthed wonder at the scene, quickly making his way passed the impaled car the uniformed man discovered Jim, "Bloody Hell mate you all right !?" he blurted out.

From his prone position Jim confirmed that he was, "Bollards saved me," he said. The uniformed man reached out and Jim transferred his weight from the bollards to him. The man pulled Jim to a standing position and looked him in the eye, "lucky escape mate" Jim smiled his agreement. The uniformed man gave Jim a simultaneous two handed pat on each shoulder and said right, I'd better make some calls" and he reached for his mobile phone.

Jim composed himself, he took another incredulous look at the car, turned to the shop and noted that despite the dramatic action a pavement's width away the premises themselves were undamaged. He reached for the shutter, pulled it down and padlocked it into place. The uniformed man returned, "okay I've got recovery on the way, if the police turn up I'll handle them, now you sure you're okay ?"

Jim looked the uniformed man in the eyes.

"Physically I am okay," he confirmed " But oh man…" Jim's eyes shot skyward.

The uniformed man gave him a reassuring punch on the shoulder, "Hey I really doubt they were trying to kill you, just saw you and kinda panicked I guess.."

"Yeah.. just kinda panicked…" repeated Jim reciprocating the man's punch to the shoulder. "Okay if you've got this I am outta here, I need to get home and have a lie down."

"Fairplay mate, I got this," confirmed the man in uniform.

Jim hurried to the tram stop, he was not aware of anything around him, he knew he was not aware of anything around him, this was a bad thing his brain confirmed, he stopped himself walking. He stood straight, hands thrusted deep into his jacket pockets, immobile, slowly he began to master his breathing. The irregular breaths gained a rhythm, in and out began matching each other in strength duration. The rhythmic intake of oxygen calmed him. He imagined the oxygen was infused with the aroma of fine marijuana and the thought made him laugh. Jim laughed for the first time since.. since.. 'Since a kid in a stolen car tried to smash into my shop with me standing in the way' was the clear and rational reply presented by his brain. Brain then followed it up with the equally rational 'and you know you're just going to have to deal with it and let it go.' 'I know' replied Jim to his brain, though he couldn't resist the final thought, 'fucking great bollards.'

Jim resumed walking without a hitch, the tram arrived within five minutes and he was at home within thirty-five and able to open the door with a smile on his face. The flat was quiet, Steve was visible seated in a chair in the lounge, he was reading and the television was off. Jim entered quietly, his brother looked up and closed his book. "No Imogen ?" questioned Jim.

"No," replied Steve, "her mother thought she best stay with her a few days."

"Aah"

"Your shop is called Legal Jims right ? James, we have the same surname, people will connect the two of us."

"Yes it is possible."

"And I am a teacher. I work with children. And a big part of taking responsibility for children is keeping them safe, keeping them away from drugs you know."

"The whole point of my shop is that we don't sell to under twenty-ones, and we really really don't."

"Yes but you do quite publically sell to adults and average people do not make the distinction, you might be a legit dealer but you are still quite literally a drug dealer. I am a school teacher, those two roles sit on opposite sides of the fence."

"Fairpoint," countered Jim, now sunk into a chair of his own, "you could publicly disown me, no hard feelings."

"I could," responded Steve," and maybe the grown-ups will buy it, but every kid that learns that Legal Jim and I are brothers will be like 'Sir well you can't say that because your brother…'"

"I get it, hey it does really seems like I'm going to make good money, you could come in with me.."

"No thank you James, I prefer to sell knowledge rather than cannabis."

Jim shut up.

"And your scheme is hampering my ability to do just that."

"I'm not giving up on this," stated Jim. "This is my first taste of success since, since we won that orienteering competition on that PGL holiday when we were kids. Legal Jims is something that is making me money, and it's also a business that's giving others an opportunity too, it's kinda exciting and I'm not letting go."

“Okay”, nodded Steve, “I understand.”

The two sat in silence for a while.

“The excitement will die down, it’s inevitable,” proffered Jim.

“Hope so” nodded Steve who quietly left the room. Jim headed to bed moments after, no spliff, no thinking he told himself, just switch off, his brain gratefully acknowledged the instruction.

Jim snapped awake Tuesday morning. His first visual thought was of the headlights suspended above his crouching form with the dirty rubber tyres spinning wildly either side, he acknowledged the thought and supressed it, he recalled the exchange with the uniformed man, which he replayed and confirmed, then the exchange with his brother, also surpassed. Jim swung his feet to the floor, right to work his brain commanded. He was washed, fed, and had donned the brown jacket and exited the flat within six hundred seconds, and was on the tram minutes later, today he noted he felt no shame in wearing the jacket.

The scene outside Legal Jim’s at eight am was chaotic. The BMW X5 was still present though now on the back of a truck, the same uniformed man was having a heated conversation with the Croydon council official who’d attended the shop three weeks prior. They were gesticulating with each other each attempting to describe their view of the damage the car could have caused. Two police officers stood on the pavement watching on disinterestedly Jim took a consolidating breath and walked in to the conversation. The council official looked up from his gesticulating and took two steps towards Jim to confirm his identity.

“Mr Pemberton,” he growled.

“Yes,” confirmed Jim, “I’m afraid I don’t recall..”

“Mr Pemberton,” the official continued, “last night a stolen vehicle was driven with great speed at your shop’s premises.”

“Yes I know,” confirmed Jim.

“Events that we predicted may well happen. We have observed your shop premises Mr Pemberton, we do know there are large queues on the street everyday, Now if hoodlums have begun to drive stolen cars up onto the pavement on the very street where those queues occur, it would be remiss of me Mr Pemberton, it would be remiss not to use my powers to prevent a tragedy occurring !”

“So under section twenty of the welfare act of nineteen thirty-one which states that an authority may suspend, or revoke, the licence of a trader if there is reason to believe it is prejudicial to the general health and welfare, and cars mounting pavements counts as dangerous to the general health and welfare Mr Pemberton ! And as this byelaw gives the local authority to suspend or revoke your licence I am suspending your licence to trade Mr Pemberton.” Having completed his tirade the council official pulled from his pocket a rolled up printed notice, and from a second pocket some sellotape and attached the notice to the shutters of Legal Jims. Jim took a quick glance at the notice, it was a written notice of what the man from Croydon council had just said. Jim glanced at the police officers who indicated with gestures that they would be supporting the official in his actions.

Jim was stupefied, he became aware his jaw was hanging open. The official and the officers turned away from him and began a discussion amongst themselves. Jim lowered his skull to meet his jaw and shook his head mournfully from side to side. He felt as if he was about to drop to his knees once more. As the strength drained from him a hand suddenly grasped onto his shoulder he looked to his left and Rob was standing there, they locked eyes, Jim gestured to the scene in front of them, Rob nodded that he was aware, they looked up. Standing on the farside of the official and the officers was The Man, he was wearing sunglasses but from his head movement Jim and Rob could deduce he was reading the notice on the shutters. When The Man’s head had stopped moving he strode past the constables and the councillor without acknowledgement and tapped Jim on the shoulder, “we need to talk’ he stated and continued with his stride. Jim and Rob followed him with their eyes. The Man stopped a few strides hence having spotted Paul, Zeke and Anthony on the far side of the road, through a single gesture The Man indicated they should all attend the regular morning meeting around the back of the shop, the boys used a variety of gestures to indicate their compliance, Jim and Rob grinned and also began making their way round the back of the shops.

“Closed after one day !” yelled out Zeke. “Ah Man the best job I ever had, the best job anyone’s ever had and it’s closed after one day !”

“Now hold on,” intoned The Man, “we are not closed yet. They gave us, hell we bought a licence to trade and they have now suspended that licence. Why ?”

“Because of the ram raid attempt last night,” stated Jim, “I was there, the bollards saved my fucking life.” Everyone present at the meeting nodded their understanding and appreciation of the event, and the bollards.

“And now,” stated The Man, “ the council suspends our licence on some health and safety grounds, that’s where we’re at.”

“They planned it.” Chimed in Paul. “I mean the street dealers were pissed, but not so pissed as to do something like this, council staged it to shut us down.”

Rob, Jim, The Man, Zeke and Anthony reviewed the statement, no-one spoke against it.

“It’s within the realms of the possibility” Rob murmured.

“Either way,” said The Man, "they’ve suspended us on the basis of health and safety and yet the bollards did their job, nothing got broken, there has to be a way of appealing against this.”

“We start getting lawyers involved and there’s an end to our profits” bemoaned Jim.

“Time is also against us,” concurred The Man, “the seeds have been laid down, a long drawn out legal fight means a lot of lost crops.”

Sighs enveloped the group, responding to the urge for something positive to be said Paul piped up, “if we could prove the council was behind the car thing their case would like collapse.”

“It ain’t the most relevant thing, but it is something” commented The Man, "okay you know people ask around see what you can find out.” Paul furtively nodded.

“Now” continued The Man, and then he stopped.

Matthew and Simon had come around the side of the building and gestured to all present, "You need to come and see this." Stated Matthew. "Now" added Simon.

Zeke, Paul, Anthony, Rob, Jim and The Man dutifully followed Matthew and Simon out of the car park, past the barrier and to the front corner of the building however they could proceed no further due to an ever increasing crowd of people amassing on the street in front of the shop. The crowd had encircled the councillor and the constables, angry shouts emerged from the amassed throng, one of the constables was talking very hurriedly into his radio and the Legal Jim crew heard sirens scream in the distance. The random shouts from the crowd became a chant, "open the shop, open the shop, open the shop." Until a thousand voices sent the slogan slamming against the cowering councillor and the stunned coppers.

A police van pulled up on the far side of the crowd and eight uniformed PCs tumbled out, they organised and formed themselves into a triangular formation and began forcing a route through the crowd towards the besieged officials at the shop doors.

Jim turned to his crew, "we do not interfere, they shut us down legally, the people are protesting for us, yes this is good but no joining in, we are Legal Jims we have to find a legal way to protest."

"Agreed" The Man concurred in his deepest tones. The group hunched together like a bunch of footballers facing gruelling added time. As they released a camera being hoisted onto a shoulder caught Jim's eye, looking across he saw Kathryn standing by the camera man. They smiled in mutual recognition and cautiously approached one another.

"Well at least this has happened before we went to press," Kathryn began," or our story would have been totally out of date, what are you going to do about it ?" "We'll be keeping it legal," smiled Jim, "Croydon council have suspended our licence on the basis of a health and safety decision, we will be appealing that decision."

“Please keep me informed,” smiled Kathryn. “Right I’m off to get some statements from the people,” she said and then disappeared into the crowd clutching notebook and pen. The newly arrived police officers had made it to the centre of the throng and joining up with their besieged colleagues formed a protective circle around the councillor, whilst imploring the crowd to calm down and disperse. The number of cameras being held up prevented Jim from seeing the results of the police protestations.

“Okay”, reported Jim ,”the police are keeping the store secure, we need to go somewhere quiet where were able to think quietly, and work out a sensible plan of action.”

“Pub ?” said Rob.

“Pub.” Concurred The Man, Matthew and Simon.

Anthony and Zeke nodded, Paul said, “I’m gonna start asking around ‘bout the car, meet you there later,” the men acknowledged his words and Paul slipped away down a side street. The remaining Legal Jim crew made their way to the town centre and took over a large round table in a sprawling blue pub that served breakfast. Simon and Matthew reached for menus, Rob asked the first question.

“Do you think he could be right ? They staged the car thing..”

“Seems like an extreme way to go about things,” breathed The Man, “Jim, what did you see ? What did you hear ?”

“I’d locked up the back of the shop,” recounted Jim, “walked out the front of the shop, shut and locked the front door, was reaching up for the shutter when I heard a young male voice shout ‘now before he closes it’, the headlights came on, the car drove straight at me and slap bang into the bollards, then after that a car door opening and footsteps running away.”

“Well that sounds like stupid scared kids then and hey man they were after getting through the shop window, they weren’t specifically trying to kill you.”

“I’d prefer if no-one killed me accidentally either.”

The men laughed. The Man continued, "And so the local council has said because of a car trying to drive on to the pavement where our queues are forming they are suspending our licence."

"They may have a point.." offered Matthew.

"I get with the safety first," responded The Man, "but that doesn't get our business open, if it takes more bollards we will get more bollards, what we need is to make a legal challenge to the council opposing their closing us, we need to know what they want to see happen to allow us to open again, and I doubt they know what that is yet."

"We need to reassure then we're co-operative, we completely agree with the need for public safety, but like you say we just don't know what measures the council will decide to ask us to put in place, and how long that decision will take."

"If Paul finds out that it was them that drove the car at Jim their case will collapse," stated Zeke excitedly.

"Highly unlikely," Intoned The Man, "but if that little conspiracy theory proves to be true the whole legal case becomes a lot more complicated while our licence remains suspended meanwhile I've got an army growers upping their production, something needs to be done." The Man looked around the group determinedly.

"I got the news," declared Anthony holding up his phone, "they're reporting the shop is shut due to an overnight incident, pictures of the BMW being taken away, and they're covering the crowd outside the shop, some of them have made banners."

"This could play out either way," proposed Jim, "the council could call out the crowd as further evidence of public disorder and keep us shut.."

"or" completed Rob, "they could listen to the crowd and let us open."

The two propositions hung in the air battling it out between themselves. Jim's phone rang, pulling it from his pocket he saw withheld number 'worked last time' he thought and answered.

"Mr Pemberton" an authoritative female voice commanded.

"Yes" confirmed Jim.

"This is Elaine from the CLA"

Jim was stunned into silence by the use of a first name,

"Elaine," he repeated hesitantly "from the cannabis licencing authority" he spelt out for the benefit of his colleagues.

"Yes Indeed," confirmed Elaine solely to Jim, "Now I'm not sure how to put this but speaking honestly I do believe it would be very much in your interests to come and see us, at the building where we had the interview, right away."

"Come and see you right away." Repeated Jim for the benefit of his agog colleagues.

"Yes well I believe your premises are closed currently are they not ?"

"They are."

"Well this is the matter we wish to discuss."

"I shall be there as soon as public transport can deliver me to your door."

"See you shortly." Elaine hung up. Jim held out the phone in stunned silence, he looked at The Man, The Man shrugged, he looked at Rob, Rob mumbled, "I dunno" None of Anthony Matthew, Simon or Zeke risked offering any advice.

"Right" said Jim, "I'm off to attend the CLA, if I don't return, avenge my death."

"Will do," said Rob cheerfully as Matthew and Simon's breakfasts arrived to a rapturous reception.

VI. The CLA

Jim hopped on to his researched route to the CLA office, arriving within thirty minutes, he made the walk from train station to building within four minutes and was skipping up the stairs a precise forty-five minutes after receiving the call. “Mr Pemberton” called out the voice behind the screen followed by a satisfied “aah” as the CLA manager, Elaine, emerged from a side door into the reception area. “Mr Pemberton, Jim” Elaine greeted him, “glad you could make it so quick.” “Well the council have shut my shop so I was at a loose end.” “Yes we are aware” confirmed Elaine, “Now if you’d like to follow me.”

Jim prepped to follow Elaine into the interview room as before but she flipped on her heel and indicated he should follow her back through the door she emerged from. Jim obliged and began trailing Elaine through the corridors of the converted police station until they reached the former cell block. Peering down to what was the cells Jim could see the steel doors had been replaced by frosted glass partitions. Elaine indicated Jim should take a seat on the raised area where a custody sergeant had once sat. Swivelling on his chair Jim noticed there was still a panel of display screens where once upon a time prisoners would have been viewed in their cells, presently the screens displayed a menu. The door to the custody ‘suite’ opened and the female engineer who’d completed the installations at Legal Jims walked in. “This is Jane,” introduced Elaine, though Jane and Jim did not shake hands. “She’s much better at these things than I,” Elaine said by way of explanation and Jane also took a seat on the dias and began connecting a laptop to the display screens. Jim waited patiently, Elaine brought her hands together and placed them on the table.

“Now Mr Pemberton, a statement of intent. Nobody in this building is for you or against you. We are civil servants we are not for or against anybody. Our aim and purpose is to see that the proper application of the laws as they apply to the selling of cannabis are applied, and we have quite a fear that the law is not being applied correctly.”

Jim was listened so intently he didn’t realise Elaine was waiting for a reaction, “please go on,” he monotoned.

Jane indicated she had established a connection between her laptop and the screens.

“Right well you’ll recall our cameras being fitted in your store last night..”

Jim nodded.

“Well they were operational from the moment Jane hooked them up, so they caught your unfortunate incident on camera, you had a lucky escape.”

Elaine pointed to the display screen and Jim saw himself locking up the store’s front door and reaching up for the shutter, then the screen became flooded in light and Jim saw himself dropping to the ground as the front bumper of the X5 shot into view from the right of the screen, before going riding up the bollards and coming crashing down on top of them. The figure of Jim remained motionless on the floor. Watching Jim knew that he had survived the incident but was still absolutely transfixed until he saw that the figure of Jim was moving and unharmed.

Elaine had a look of shocked sympathy on her face, Jane began running forward the camera feed, Jim composed himself adding, “I am so glad we took official advice on those bollards.”

Elaine smiled. She waited until Jane had run the video on to eight o’clock in the morning when the figure of the Croydon councillor could be seen sellotaping his notice to the shutter doors. “Mmm, yes now this little incident” she muttered.

“I do understand the point of view..” began Jim preparing to list his objections however Elaine interrupted him before he could get going.

“Yes of course we are all very much concerned with public safety however it is the proper application of the law that we are most concerned with here, do you recall what legal power the councillor used to close your shop ?”

Jim searched his memory.. “The Welfare Act…? He tentatively suggested. “Well remembered Mr Pemberton,“ commentated Elaine, “The Welfare Act 1931 as is written here on his notice,” she said indicating the live feed from the Legal Jim shop camera. Jim leaned in to read the writing and confirmed Elaine’s statement.

“And…” Questioned Jim.

"There is no Welfare Act nineteen thirty-one, it does not exist. What we believe he must be referring to is the Children and Young Persons Act of nineteen thirty-one, which does exist and yes this Act gives the local authority the power, well let me give you chapter and verse, to suspend or revoke a street trader's licence if it has reason to believe that the holder's continued employment in street trading would be prejudicial to his health, welfare or ability to take full advantage of his education.

Jim raised his eyebrows.

"The Act is there to protect children employed by street traders Mr Pemberton, and you are not a street trader and not in need of having your education protected. Also these byelaws were revoked in nineteen seventy-three. Croydon council have no legal basis whatsoever for shutting you down."

Jim was stunned, he didn't speak. He gestured with his hands firstly at the screen and then displaying both palms up he mouthed the words well what can I do.

"If Croydon council wish do wish to close you down they are quite able to follow the proper legal channels by applying to a court, the current situation will not stand. I have informed the minister of what has occurred, I'll be honest Mr Pemberton Croydon council haven't answered our calls all morning so I have asked for the minister to contact the councillor directly. This should have happened in the last half hour and oh yes," confirmed Elaine idling flicking to an e-mail arrived on the laptop, "the councillor confirms he will meet you at your premises at three o'clock to officially rescind his revocation of your licence, we must let him have his little sense of occasion mustn't we ?"

"Indeed we must," accepted Jim.

Elaine looked at Jim brimming with prim correctness, the error in law enforcement had been corrected, the parties had been informed, her job was most completely complete. Jim didn't know if a thank you was appropriate, Elaine certainly did not seem to be trying to elicit one, Jim opted for a nod., the most courteous and thoughtful nod he could manage, Elaine acknowledged it with a blink.

Jim rose from his seat and Elaine completed their exchange with, “Jane will see you out.” Jane rose from her seat and opened the former custody suite door, Jim followed her through. There was no talk as they made their back through the corridors to the lobby, she opened the door from him, Jim raised his hand in thanks and exited the innards of the CLA. “Goodbye Mr Pemberton” said the voice behind the screen, “bye” replied Jim back to the void and he swiftly left the building. He crossed the street to be out of range of the cameras he knew surrounded the building and having turned a corner he found the nearest wall and leant against it.

Jim reviewed recent events. Near death experience followed by nightmare morning and now, quite probably, a way of waking from that nightmare at three pm, Jim glanced at his phone to check the time, whistled in shock and began running for the train station.

He was delivered back to Croydon with twenty minutes to spare and hurriedly made his way to the shop. There were the remnants of a crowd outside, a few people were posing with phones in front of the shut shutters and transmitting their pictures with a crying face emoji. Two police officers stood by a police van parked across the street from shop Jim waited for a pause in the photo taking and them moved in front of the doors, producing the shop keys out from his brown jacket pocket.

The amassed influencers and instagrammers took note, Jim held his pose keys in hand, one of the phone totters shouted out, “Hey Mister You re-opening ?” “Probably” was Jim’s reply. There was ‘whoop-whoop’ in reply. The group’s attention was drawn by a white council van that pulled up beside the police van. The by now familiar shape of the Croydon council official emerged awkwardly from the car and spoke briefly with the police officers who joined him in making their way across the street to speak to Jim in front of the shop.

The officers safely delivered the official to the shop front, he and Jim faced each other, neither was inclined to speak though the officials need for officiousness won out. “It appears that I was remiss in my use of the legal powers which I cited in order to suspend your licence however….” The official held up his finger however no words emerged from his mouth to join with the gesture, after a while his finger began wavering.

“You were acting with the best interests of public safety in mind…” suggested Jim helpfully.

“I was.” Confirmed the official, “I was,” and with those words the rest of his fingers joined the first one in pulling the sellotaped notice off Legal Jim’s shutter doors. Satisfied he had removed all traces of the notice the official addressed Jim directly, “good day to you sir !” He stated and hurried off towards his van. “Good day,” said Jim gently to the officials retreating form, the police officers melted away and Jim was faced with a most agitated and expectant crowd. He faced them, “I need my staff” he explained. The crowd nodded. Jim reached for his phone and pressed dial on The Man’s number. The Man answered. “Shop’s open.” Stated Jim. The Man’s whoop was heard by the crowd. Jim smiled and closed his phone. He smiled at the customers. “The shop will open in ten or fifteen minutes, half an hour at the most as soon as the staff arrive.” The crowd sighed collectively and contentedly. With the grammers and the fluencers at the front an impromptu press conference arose, “Why did they close you down ?” called out a voice.

“There was an incident here last night“, replied Jim pointing to the damage to the bollards.

“What happened ?” asked a second voice.

“Someone tried to ram raid the shop”, explained Jim.

“Good bollards” said another voice.

“Good bollards” confirmed Jim.

“Did they catch them ?”

“Don’t know” said Jim, “haven’t heard as yet.”

As the crowd retreated into itself to try and think up more questions Jim's eyes were drawn to a sight beyond the crowd. The Legal Jim staff were approaching. The Man led the way, Rob, Anthony and Zeke walked behind bedecked in their brown jackets, besuited Matthew and Simon were at the rear walking awarely scanning the crowd. Jim grinned. The crew was here, the crowd parted. The staff of Legal Jims walked through to rapturous applause. Jim and The Man laid eyes upon each other first, "How ?" Asked The Man. "Oh do I have a tale for you !" Smiled Jim rolling up the shutters.

The staff were cheered one by one as they entered the shop, the customer registration machines had never been off, the display lights were switched on, Rob, Anthony and Zeke took their places behind the counter, Matthew and Simon joined The Man and Jim on the street and began influencing the formation of a queue, The Man addressed the crowd, "We are open !" He declared, the crowd went wild !

Rob, Anthony and Zeke had taken up their positions behind the counter, Rob nodded affirmatively to Simon, who are glanced at Matthew further down the street, he nodded, and Simon opened the shop doors. The customers eagerly passed in past The Man and Jim who smiling reassuringly strolled behind the counter and slid through the door at the back, they crouched into instant attentive conversation.

"What happened ?" asked The Man.

"Croydon council shut us down illegally." Stated Jim, "the cameras right ? They caught everything the beamer hitting the bollards, me ducking, and the notice the bloke from Croydon council stuck on the shutters, and that notice right stated the legal powers used to shut us down, and they were well out of date, repealed, revoked, whatever, and the CLA was very concerned by like the illegal legal activity, they got their minister to call the council and voila we are open !"

The Man's jaw dropped revealing his perfect teeth, he beamed the most magnificent smile and he and Jim successfully fist-bumped. There was a loud desperate knocking at the backdoor.

Jim went to the back door, "who dere !?" he demanded.

"Paul" came the informative reply.

Jim opened the door and ushered him in, bolting it firmly behind him. Paul nodded to The Man and Jim and spoke, “Right I think I know who was driving the car.”

“Do you know know or do you think you know ?”

“No I don’t know know for sure but I ‘m pretty sure I know.”

“Go on” interjected The Man hurriedly.

“Well like I said it wasn’t a member of the association of street dealers I asked ‘em all face to face like and everyone said no”

“Well durr” interrupted Jim.

“But Shifty Jack seriously reckoned it was Big Dom. So Shifty Jack is a member of the association, Big Dom is not, but Big Dom does run errands for Shifty Jack, and he’s always had a thing for BMWs and knows his way around the locks for sure, Jack’s tried to beep him this morning, no reply.”

“Promising” confirmed The Man, “very promising, but not enough for a conviction.”

“Well Big Dom is the sort of bloke nobody likes,” continued Paul.

“Because of his size ?” queried Jim.

“Because of his smell,” confessed Jim, ”don’t know if he tries to do anything about it, but really not good, no no-one wants him in the association but like through Shifty Jack he was associated, and I do remember him being well pissed when you, er now we, like totally we guys, opened up.”

“Certainly a suspect, do you know anymore ? Who he associates with ? Where he hangs ?” Asked The Man, turning to Jim, “there were two of them right ?”

Jim nodded his confirmation, “must have been, one driving the car, the other voice came from a different direction from the car.”

The Man turned to Paul, “You’ve got my number, good work so far, if you do learn where he’s at call me first okay, I would like to ask him a few questions directly.”

"Will do" confirmed Paul, Jim unbolted the back door and Paul slipped out. In the quiet that followed Jim asked The Man, " what do we gain by tracking him down ?" "We make sure he never tries it again, "replied The Man. Jim had no come back.

The business partners returned to the front of their shop, the customers had remained eager, the staff were swift and courteous and security was in place. Legal Jims hummed. As the afternoon progressed the conversation turned to the hour the shop would stay open to, we regularly offer an eight hour nine to five service mused Jim, so three to eleven would seem reasonable was the proposition he put to the staff, with the promise of an anti-social hours bonus payment, which all the staff readily agreed to. So on the ninth day of trading Legal Jims stayed open late into the night, staff and customers traded stories of the finest dopes they had ever smoked and the shop hummed with vitality, until a strange odour began to drift into the store.

One by one the people in the store, led by their noses, looked up. Simon on the door was the first to spot something unusual, Paul was standing on the far side of the street adjacent to a very large male. Jim was able to connect the sight with the smell and indicated as clearly as he could that Paul and his friend should go around the building to the back of the store.

Jim and The Man exited the back of the shop so as to meet Paul and the man they could only assume to be Big Dom out in the fresh air.

"That's far enough." Stated The Man as Paul and Big Dom approached, addressing Paul directly he demanded, "What is going on ?"

"Right" began Paul "Well I found Big Dom and he was like really apologetic, he really wanted to say sorry in person.."

"Exactly that !" Blurted out Big Dom, he looked at Jim, "I am so sorry man I never meant to drive at you, we just wanted in to the shop."

"Tell me exactly what happened." Commanded Jim as best he could.

"Well me and my mate we was well pissed at you, no word of a lie, coming round here nicking all our business and well my mate right said it would be a good idea to ram raid your shop and nick all your gear and sell that, win win. Anyway so we went and nicked the car right and parked up opposite your shop, saw that there were lots of lights on and people fitting stuff so we decided to wait, anyway I'd had a smoke, engine was on, car was warm and I fell asleep, and when me mate woke me up shouting 'do it now', I just slammed down on the speed, wrenched the wheel to the right and a moment later I was stuck on your bollards. "

Jim locked his stare on Big Dom and took steps towards him, sniffed the air, thought better about it, and took three steps back.

Big Dom looked at Jim understandingly, "I just really wanted to say sorry mate, we only meant to smash up your shop, not you."

Jim gave no reply.

"You say we" interceded The Man, "who's your mate ?"

"Shifty Jack" replied Big Dom.

"I knew it !" Exploded Paul slamming his fist into his palm.

"You gonna try doing it again ? Smashing up out store ?"

"Might do, " tendered Big Dom, "word is you've got the best shit."

It was clear to Paul and Jim that The Man fully prepared to lay into Big Dom fists first. Big Dom was wide but The Man was taller and had the appearance of being all muscle, Big Dom appeared to be mainly blubber. Though Big Dom's natural defence was clearly working as The Man remained at arm's length and spoke softly and clearly.

"Who do you mainly sell to Dom ?"

"Schoolkids mostly."

"We do not sell to schoolkids, we are not your competition."

Dom let out a vague, "uh huh"

“Who else do you know who sells to schoolkids ?” Inquired The Man gently.

“Shifty Jack” confirmed Dom instantaneously, ”and a couple of others.”

“Well then I think you have identified who your true competition is,” concluded The Man.

“Yeah” nodded Big Dom, looking around for confirmation he saw Jim and Phil nodding vigorously.

“School kids wouldn’t appreciate our shit anyway” grinned The Man, ”So is it fair to say we won’t be experiencing anymore visits from you right, we are not in competition with each other, we can peacefully co-exist.”

“We can peacefully co-exist” echoed Jim and Paul in a chant-like manner.

“We can peacefully co-exist” repeated Big Dom dutifully.

Big Dom turned to leave though was hauled back by some words from The Man.

“And hey I’d keep a close eye on Shifty Jack if I were you, “ The Man gave a knowing wink and enacted a playful double punch.

Big Dom winked in return and then faded away into the night, his smell lingered.

The Man, Jim and Paul retreated into the back of the shop.

“Well I think that’s the best that could be done, “suggested The Man, Jim and Paul nodded,” I really don’t think we’ll be seeing anymore of Big Dom. But if we do……we’ll smell him a mile off.”

Paul groaned, Jim shook his head in despair.

“Listen,” said the man changing the subject, “how long we got to go tonight ?”

“ ’bout an hour left.” Confirmed Jim.

“Okay you will be fine and I’m gonna skedaddle,” stated The Man, “I like to be there for bedtime reading, “ he beamed, “we’ve just started Harry Potter.”

“We will be fine,” confirmed Jim, ”also Paul take the rest of the night mate, bloody good detective work mate, really appreciated, see you for normal hours and a normal day tomorrow.”

Paul smiled appreciatively as he slipped out the door after The Man.

Paul slid into the front of the shop, Rob, Anthony and Zeke were doing their thing, only Matthew of Matthew and Simon remained on duty and he appeared most at ease. Jim began helping out at the till and indicated Anthony and Zeke could leave for the day, "extra pay for today, normal day tomorrow" he noted, the boys thanked hung up their jackets and left. As the queue outside dwindled Matthew retreated back into the shop. Jim swiftly asked, "hey mate after last night, would you mind walking me to the tram stop ?" "Not at all boss," Matthew warmly replied. Rob and Jim cheerfully served the last few customers who gratefully grasped each one of their purchases, sharing many mischievous grins with Rob and Jim in return.

The late closure went smoothly and having padlocked down the shutters Rob and Jim happily skipped along either side of Matthew down to the tram stop and all parties were able to leave the borough of Croydon without incident.

Jim returned to an empty flat, he thought little of it and banishing all thoughts he could of recent events collapsed into sleep. It was only in the morning he noticed the note on the coffee table.

'James,

It's your brother here, I've gone. My rent is taken care of until the end of the month, it sounds as if you will have no problem taking care of things after that. It's just like that movie Tequila Sunrise, okay so that was a cop and a coke dealer, and we are a teacher and a legal marijuana seller, but the principle is the same it just doesn't work. I've got myself a place closer to school, please try and keep our name out of events and I'll see you at Mums for Christmas,

Stephen.'

Jim sat in quiet contemplation, he tried to equate himself with a man who's wife had left him, but having never had a wife he found it a difficult thought to muster. He couldn't feel properly sad because he knew it was absolutely the right decision in the circumstances, but it did feel sad, it was a sad situation, though Jim knew the only thing he could do to make it better was to totally keep his distance from his family, the best thing he could give them was his absence, and that was a sad thought.

"Oh well" thought Jim, "At least I can smoke indoors now."

Jim grabbed the sacred box from his room and laid out grinder, papers (the good kind with the cardboard tips), tobacco, the finest bud his store could provide, lighter and ashtray. He crossed his legs up on the sofa laid his back against the upright cushion and contemplated the objects for a short while, making sure none of them moved. They didn't. So Jim had to move them himself. He extracted the top paper with the utmost care and laid it out in front of him, ensuring that the paper lay perfectly parallel with the table's edge. He loving created a bed of tobacco upon the paper on which to lay the bud, and casually rolled a small piece of cardboard into a cylinder between his thumb and first finger, placing it pillow like at the head of the tobacco. He burst open the plastic baggy containing the bud nasily inhaling its' glorious contents, he held the bud over the tobacco and eased a piece off from the main body of the plant, ensuring that anything falling leaves would land securely in the tobacco. Taking his piece of bud he pressed it deeply into the cogs of the grinder and clicked down the lid, he swivelled the grinder using both hands as if it were a cocktail shaker, he brought it once up to his right shoulder, once to his left, then brought it down to about an inch above the tobacco and pulled it oh so gently apart. The ground marijuana fell like snow onto the tobacco ground. Jim placed the grinder to one side and smiled upon his creation, he took some more tobacco from the pouch and laid it on top of the ground marijuana ensuring that it was all covered up. Once satisfied no green was peeking through Jim tapped the cylindrical pillow against the tobacco bed and smiled benignly. He leant the protruding part of the paper against the second and third fingers of each hand, pressed forward his thumbs to hold everything in place, licked, and then raised and rolled the spliff in a flowing simultaneous action. The roll complete Jim added the daintiest little fuse. The finished product looked smoother than a space rocket, many rolls get called perfect thought Jim, this one certainly sits among them. Jim hesitated in lighting it, he twirled the perhaps perfect joint around before his eyes appreciating its' flawless quality. Jim reached for his lighter, he didn't need to look, he knew where it was, and he flipped it up and he lit the fuse, Jim smiled.

His deep inhalations of satisfaction took him many places. He began with the review of where he was at. Well hey, here he was managing Britain's first legal dope shop and somehow someway he had kept it open for the first full nine days of trading, this was a good thing. If you think things are good something's wrong responded his mind. Hey ain't nothing wrong right now, just be thankful for that Jim's brain retorted. Well his mind replied what about the opium wars, since you stem from a culture that fought two wars from 1839-42 and 1856-60 to gain the power to distribute dope to a foreign country you can hardly say you run Britain's first legal shop.

Ah hah smokin' Jim responded to his mind but they did outlaw opium dens from nineteen twenty onwards, and it's only now it's been relegalised, I am not the British East India Company, I don't work that way, I am something new. Fairplay replied his mind and smokin' Jim and his brain agreed it was best they didn't talk anymore.

Jim slept where he smoked. He slept well and woke naturally an hour before he needed to be at the shop, he reminded himself why he was able to sleep so freely on the crouch, grimaced slightly and headed for the bathroom.

Day ten of business at Legal Jims and Jim swept in to the morning meeting, Rob was alert, The Man was stoic, Matthew and Simon surveyed the surrounding area, Paul, Anthony and Zeke rolled the joints. Paul displayed his most magnificent multi-papered six inch rocket first, muttering the obligatory, 'now that gentlemen is a camberwell carrot', the appreciation was clear to see in Anthony and Zeke's eyes. Zeke was the next to unveil his creation, equally slender along the stem but expanding into a spherical fuse constructed of pure bud, 'proper bifter' he commented, Anthony and Paul nodded. Finally Anthony revealed his creation, he placed his hand in front of him fingertips at the top, wrist at the bottom, palm inwards fingers facing the group and with other his hand brought his spliff up the palm gradually revealing the finished creation over the tops of his fingers. It rose above his finger nails, it kept on rising and kept on rising, eight inches at the very least, with a two inch roach keeping the shape of the cylinder utterly perfect down the entire length of its' shaft. Paul and Zeke very very carefully laid down their spliffs in safe places and broke into rapturous applause. Matthew and Simon glanced on admiringly, Rob whooped, Jim circled his right fist in the air. And The Man nodded approvingly.

Anthony offered his creation to The Man, The Man clearly shook his head and gestured for Anthony to light it. Zeke took his and presented it to Jim, who was hesitant, but a go on nod from Zeke led Jim into taking on responsibility for the bifter. Paul offered Rob his spliff, Rob took it. As the joints were lit Matthew and Simon gathered in and the morning meeting commenced.

Time passed.

It was a quiet meeting, nothing was said, there were a few sounds of inhalation, the odd cough, and a fair amount of nodding appreciation.

After more time had passed one member of the group, it was unclear who, held up a phone displaying the time, it took a few moments, maybe seconds, maybe minutes, maybe longer but gradually everyone came to the realisation that yes a digital display of the time was being shown, there was some nodding.

A voice spoke, “we should..” A muttered voice replied, “we should.”

The rear door to Legal Jim’s emporium was opened, Paul, Anthony and Zeke were heartedly congratulated on their joint rolling prowess and the crew of the shop drifted into work.

At nine am the doors were flung open to cheers from the crowd, Matthew and Simon started out blankly and benignly and the customers soon realised they’d better form a queue, and best do it themselves. As the first eager purchases filed into the shop the rest of the staff Jim, Anthony, Rob, Paul and Zeke were all leaning very comfortably against the back wall, Zeke managed a wave, the understanding customers began very carefully tiptoeing around the shop.

After a spot of perusing the first customer arrived at the counter. Anthony was standing by the till but he wasn’t really there, the customer turned to Rob who shuffled across, slowly, he arrived, remembered why he was there, and broke into a wide shopkeeper’s grin. “Whatever you choose…” He began, “I recommend really taking time with your roll.”

The customer expressed his appreciation at the wisdom of Rob's words. Jim sensing there was need for his senses eased his way between Rob and Zeke and also adopting a shopkeepers smile addressed the customer with a cheery, "and what will you be having sir ?" "vanilla cake" came the informed reply.

With the first seal of a bag and beep of the machine the business day began, slowly the staff lifted from their stupor, Matthew and Simon standing out in the open air started recovering from the morning meeting first, Simon was betwixt the bollards and door, Matthew further down the street where customers were joining the queue. Both spotted the man across the street, a man taller than either of them, dressed in dark clothes and dark glasses standing on the far pavement and taking a long lasting deeply contemplative look at Legal Jims. Matthew glanced at Simon confirming the sighting, Simon in turn stared directly at the man, initially stoically, then inquisitively and receiving no reaction Simon then shook his head dismissively. Matthew left his spot at the end of the queue and strode down the length of the queue. "Don't like the look of this" he muttered to Simon as he passed him and entered the shop.

The Man was behind the counter as Matthew entered the shop, Matthew grabbed his attention with a "here boss" and The Man joined Matthew at the window where he brought The Man's attention to the man across the street. The movement caught Jim's eye and looking across at the two men he saw The Man's face drop, Jim skipped across to join them, The Man turned to Matthew. "Okay I know the face, do not engage him, resume your positions and keep an eye, if you can note when he leaves and who he leaves with, this visit is probably just a warning, but keep your wits about you." Matthew confirmed his comprehension and hurried outside to relay the instructions to Simon. The Man turned to Jim, "a word if I may.." his first finger pointing to the back room. Jim followed him through firmly shutting the door to the shop behind him and spoke first, "Trouble ?"

"Trouble."

"Who he ?"

"It's not so much him as who he represents, what he represents."

"Something big ?"

"Some big people."

"I'll bet."

"Jim we come from very different worlds. What were you, fifteen years a jeweller ?"

"Something like that."

"And in that time when any other jeweller got successful, made a good sale, did you and a bunch of other jewellers get together and go round and smash up their shop and nick their stuff."

"No actually, no, we never did that."

"Happens in my world."

"Ah hah"

"Now a quick history lesson for you, I have been selling dope for decades, when I first realised there was always going to be demand, and that I knew exactly where the supply was, and that there were no taxes, and the profits were only limited by the amount you could shift, man I went to work, and I went to work big, and selling dope has paid for my life, it has paid for my wife, it pays for my daughter, selling mary jane gives me a nice life, I love mary jane, she loves me back, all good man but there are of course many other folks who have had the same realisation and they have also had the realisation that there are no rules to dope selling, ain't no fucker going to the police, so if some of these individuals decide to hurt the other dealers and take their stuff there's fuck all that can be done about it. Now a while back a few of these malicious individuals got together and formed themselves a cartel, learned themselves some economics, pooled their resources, and now they employ other people to go out and do the robbing and the violence for them, and that huge fucker out there is one of those people."

Jim nodded forlornly, "How do you deal with them ?" He asked.

"I don't"

Jim didn't reply.

"I avoid them. I sell to my customers, they sell to theirs, I get from my growers, they try fucking hard to find out where my growers at only some of the boys in the cartel they know me, we grew up together, they know where I live, they know who my wife is, they know who my daughter is, and if they've decided to come after me, they'll come after them, my weak spots."

Jim remained in stunned silence.

"Man the situation's been brewing for a while though so has been my solution, the wife is out in Jamaica right now scouting for properties. No way am I saying that Jamaica is safer than London but at least there the bad guys ain't looking for us. But that still leaves us here, my daughter at school and that huge fucking motherfucker standing across the street from our window. "

Jim concurred and felt helpless, he thought of all the security he had arranged for the shop and how bloody useless it was in the face of this threat, he knew he was simply not physically capable of fighting against any assailant let alone a henchmen employing cartel, the vitality drained from him and he thought of the empty room he had sat in last night and that became a sad thought which joined together with the despairing thought of having his business taken from by violent thugs and Jim slumped, he slumped in body and face and fell backwards against the wall sliding his spine downwards until he could go no lower, he tried to think but his mind had just became the same empty desolate room, that's all his life was empty, empty and vulnerable.

An empty room.

"An empty room."

"An empty room ?" Repeated The Man questioningly.

"An empty room." Stated Jim.

"An empty room." Repeated The Man staring directly eyeball to eyeball at Jim.

Jim received The Man's stare held it and returned it directly at him.

"Who am I ?" Demanded Jim.

"Eh ?"

"Who am I ?" Repeated Jim clearly.

"I dunno," responded The Man.

“Exactly ! I am nobody. To the men who are prepared to hurt your daughter I am nobody, I am unrecognisable. The empty room part, last night I went home to an empty flat, I used to live with my brother and his daughter, he’s a teacher, she’s thirteen, and he’s decided he and her cannot be around me a marijuana seller however legitimate, which means I have a flat already set up to house a young lady, your ‘friends’ have never seen me, and how do they go about tracing me, business records, CLA have been pretty damn sharp as far as I can see, what I’m saying unless they’ve already seen us working together there’s no easy way to connect our identities, while your wife’s away Man I am happy to give safe haven to your daughter.”

The Man looked at Jim with respect and gratitude, he patted his shoulder and gave him a four fingered pinch.

“A definite possibility,” he declared. “I need to see the property first, check the environment and the security.”

Jim gave two slow nods.

“Now” stated The Man, giving Jim a further pat on the same shoulder, “We are going to have to decide what to do about the man mountain that has taken up residence outside our shop.

“Well..” began Jim hesitantly, “what are his weak spots ?”

“’I’ll say one thing for sure,” replied The Man, “He don’t have no wife and kids, ain’t no way there’d be any food left over for them.”

“You say he’s a henchmen, can we out pay them ?”

“Nah man he’s too ingrained, if he flipped over to us he’d have to face all of them.”

“So he stands there and scares us until he decides to smash his way into the shop, and he looks a lot more capable than the last guy.”

“You want to pop out there and ask him to move on ?”

Jim didn't reply to The Man, he'd had an idea, thought/word thought/word he began spelling it out, "Wait, now you said the cartel robs dealers because they have no-one to complain to, and now they want to rob us"

"Yes" concurred The Man.

"But what just happened ? Croydon fookin' council just tried to close us down and the crowd, the public, our customers caused a kerfuffle and we were open back up within the day."

"I thought you said it was because Croydon council used the wrong law"

"Yeah there's that but also because they watch the news, everyone was watching and it had to be sorted out. If we go as public as fookin' possible and say hey look at our shop, we're here all the time the cartel will be unable to strike at us."

"Hold on there promo man, just a moment ago you said I am nobody, and why being nobody is a good thing, now you're saying you want to jump about in front of the cameras going I'm here I'm here."

"Not me personally, listen we get your daughter safe, double check our locks yes, but it's that bit about regular drug dealers having no recourse, were legal, we do, cartel wants to rob us, let's keep the light shining on Legal Jims as brightly as we possibly can, criminals like creeping about in darkness right, let's up our wattage."

"Okay you lost me a bit there."

"Oh you get it, keep a high profile, literally, keep the shop in the spotlight, Anthony, Paul and Zeke are young, they must have friends on tiktok get something going on social media, I now know a newspaper journalist, I can offer her stories, do everything we can to maintain a presence so we're like… or at least we look like… we're too big to rob from."

The Man chewed on Jim's words. "It's a plan" he confirmed, "right, let's get up to date on current events." Reinvigorated by their conversation the two men left the back of shop and weaved their way through the milling customers to join Simon on the pavement, Matthew had resumed position further down the street, man mountain was still in place.

"Okay" reported The Man to Simon and Jim, "I'm going to try an engagement. Matt, Si, stay on your toes, Jim please have your phone camera zoomed in and focused on me and the fellah, right I'm gonna go say hello."

The Man strode across the street, he was easily six foot himself, the brown overcoat of Legal Jim's fell elegantly across his shoulders, raybans concealed his eyes, and at this moment he felt like a cowboy, though he sorely wished he had a real pair of six shooters hung at his waist. The man he was facing, the man mountain, was somewhere over six foot seven, it was difficult to tell, black camouflage trousers and shirt, eyes also shielded by sunglasses but a far cheaper pair than The Man's.

"Hello" began The Man.

Man mountain didn't move.

"You've been watching my store and my customers for quite some time," continued The Man mirroring man mountain's pose and looking back across at the shop and the queue.

"Jealous ?" Asked The Man.

Man mountain snorted bull-like.

"Yeah business is good, now what's your interest ?"

The Man turned from facing the shop to directly confronting the mountain. He flung open his coat and placed his hands where his guns should be. The mountain slowly shifted to face The Man, the mountain spoke.

"Either we take fifty percent or we take it all."

The Mountain indicated with not inconsiderably sized fingers that taking it all meant the shop bursting into flame.

"First the business message, you and the cartel are taking nothing from me, I am not offended by your actions but now move the fuck along. Now the personal message dickhead, because you have personally have just proved to me a very specific point. You see criminals right, that is you by the way, differ from legit business men, which is me by the way, in that criminals use violence, they murder, they attack, they destroy, and then run away, except for one, there's one type of crim that comes back and takes a look at what they've done, the fuckin' arsonist. Now you have just threatened to burn my shop, oh it was caught on camera, and so if anything happens to my shop everyone will know exactly where to look and you will not be hard to find."

"But I haven't burnt your shop yet."

"And I'd call that a threat to destroy property right there, and that too, caught on camera, you should watch your lips and fingers mate, they're fucking noticeable, we're legit my friend, the police will listen to us, you start messing and you are entering a world of shit, legitimate shit, so take my advice, turn around go back to your car fucking tel and hey maybe go open up your own legal shops, there's nothing for you here."

The Man's hands were squarely on his hips, arms triangled either side, his stare locked securely upon the eyes of the man mountain looking for a response to his ultimatum. From his elevated position man mountain contemplated The Man, he brought a mobile phone up to his face and pressed one button, then dropped the phone back into a trouser pocket, his arms hanging at his side reflecting The Man's pose. Neither man spoke, the ultimatum remained unanswered, a van pulled up alongside the pair and an average sized male, also dressed in black camouflage, leapt out and took up a stance by the rear doors.

“I’ll remember your words,” rumbled the man mountain, and with that he turned, the companion opened the van doors and the mountain climbed in. The driver shut the doors and without a glance at the Man leapt back into the driver’s seat and started moving away the mountain.

The Man, looked across to Simon and Matthew, a series of double nods communicated that it was safe to stand down, Jim held his phone up with one hand and gave a thumbs up with the other, The Man gave out a long whistling sigh. He checked the traffic ever so carefully before crossing back to Mathew , Simon and Jim, a fair few members of the queue had seemed to notice the exchange as well but they kept their heads down as the big men conferred.

“What do you think ?” Asked Mathew.

“I have given them the message.” Stated The Man, “I am confident that he will take it back to them, that we are legitimate, that they can fuck off and that they will get a robust fucking response if they do try anything.”

The nod confirming the appreciation of the message delivery from Jim, Matthew, and Simon was delivered with perfect synchronicity.

“I do reckon we should continue with part two of the plan, Jim you mentioned a journalist, Matt, Si ‘ave a word with Paul, Tony and Zeke, what we want via their friends on social media is a very public message that Legal Jims is out there, this is where it’s at, we’re loud and we’re proud, and hopefully it will make it a lot harder for the cartel to do their dirty deeds if everybody’s looking. Now James you mentioned a safehouse for my daughter, please lead the way, Matt, Si, you got this ?”

Nods.

Jim and The Man headed to the tram stop, Matthew and Simon conferred, Simon went inside to pass on the message, Matthew remained outside at the head of the queue martialling the crowd and scanning the opposing pavement for any return of the mountain.

VII. A Second Meal

Jim and The Man walked swiftly and silently, the tram was too packed for them to converse. It was a short walk from the far tram stop to Jim's flat, during which time he became preoccupied with what state he had left it in the night before, he couldn't remember, he stopped trying. Trepidatiously he opened the door, and with good reason, the contents of his sacred box were still laid out artistically across the surface of the coffee table. The Man smiled, his eye took in the arrangement and the quality of the arranged articles and he nodded approvingly, "shall we ? " He asked.

"We shall" replied Jim, who gestured for The Man to take the chair while he resumed his traditional cross legged pose on the couch. "I'll roll you talk," Jim suggested, then interrupted himself, "no wait, first the plan, Jim reached for his phone, scrolled through the contacts for Kathryn and quickly typed, 'Hi it's Jim of Legal Jims here, I wanted to know if you'd like to be kept updated on developments at the shop, there's been a few, perhaps another meal, on me this time, please let me know your thoughts, Jim" He re-read it checking for politeness and punctuation, and satisfied on both counts he pressed send. Jim resumed rolling.

"Well" began Man, "we are definitely in a good place, we just don't know yet how the bad people are gonna react to us being in a good place."

Jim affirmed his understanding as he began carefully aligning two separate papers against the edge of the table.

"Flat looks secure," said The Man, "and as you said they do not know of its' location. I will not as yet go through the trauma of upsetting my girls routine by moving her in, but it is very good to know it's here, I do appreciate it."

Jim nodded.

"Now the business, the business is good, and if we really can use publicity to protect ourselves from the cartel, there ain't nothing stopping us my man, we is going places, pretty soon we'll be opening a chain of shops, setting ourselves up some franchising shit, hitting the big time."

Jim did not nod. He paused from his rolling, laid his back against the sofa and shook his head from side to side. The Man raised his eyebrows.

"I don't want to be the British East India Company."

"Come again"

"In China in the eighteen hundreds the UK fought and won two wars for the right to sell opium to the people. So that's our country threatening and killing people in another country for the right to intentionally start a drug epidemic in their country."

"So the British Empire was nasty, yes, yes it was, but how does that shit effect our shit ?"

"If we start a chain of dope shops two hundred years later that is us doing exactly the same thing, we're doing the nasty. China went on to describe those wars as part of their century of humiliation, forming a big business and forcing drugs on people, well that's what the Americans do, not us, not the British, now running one little dope shop, where eager wanting customers, all confirmed as being sane sober and over twenty-one, are queueing up to try pleasures they've never tried before, Man, that is exactly where I want to be, I'm your shopkeep, but being a big business mass selling dope to a mass market who doesn't really get it, no that's not where I want to be."

"Ethics man I get that but we don't trick nobody into our shop, they enter of their own free will, and we do check their safe, I ain't got no problem with rolling out that system."

"I suppose I like being boutique, and seriously should we be everywhere, on every corner ? Nah man it's just not…" Jim thought for a moment, "…responsible"

"And I'm the parent" grinned the Man, "Okay, no chain of franchisees as yet, but it is something to bear in mind you know, for the moment let's carry on making sure our shop stays in business."

"Aye to that" agreed to Jim perfecting and presenting the first of his spliffs to The Man.

The Man cheerfully acknowledged its receipt repaying with the broadest of grins whilst Jim continued with constructing a second spliff.

The Man spoke and The Man smoked.

“Considerate as your position is, historically speaking, there’s no particular cause to have that much of a bias towards the Chinese, after all it is themselves who first introduced humanity to the magical herb. There is of course much speculation about when mankind first made use of marijuana…”

“I heard the jewish priests were the first to use it, about two thousand seven hundred years ago, got themselves stoned, went ooh look at me I’ve seen god and religion was born,” interrupted Jim.

“Well that does pre-date mine,” admitted The Man, “I had two thousand five hundred years ago at the Jirzankal cemetery in the Pamir mountains in western China where apparently the practice was to burn the ‘erb at funerals and so ease the pain of grief. Now I have also read, same as you said, that traces of the holy herb has been found in the bowls of priests, only I was reading it was the zoroatrians not the jews, same story, different religion, however what is known is that the sacred plant did in fact originate on the Tibetan plateau, that is botanical fact. It is known to have been farmed by the Chinese four thousand years ago to make rope and paper, and it is strongly suspected that once the intoxicating strain of the plant was discovered it was distributed along the silk road, which ran for some fifteen hundreds years, so who’s the biggest dealer, you tell me.. So sure the ‘erb has been used badly, but my man, what matters is that we use the herb wisely.”

Jim completed The Man’s words, he contemplated his spliff, he raised it like a glass and touched it in a toast against The Man’s spliff, lent back, lit it and inhaled, closed his eyes, and did his utmost to really feel the dope.

“Wisdom” he concurred.

Jim and The Man remained quiet and contemplative, they did not lapse into a stupor, they sat with a quiet awareness, calm, silent, breathing in the world around them, breathing in their thoughts, pleasantly, undisturbedly, thinking. Jim's phone beeped. He didn't reach for it straight away, he'd forgotten where it was, though after a little patting down it reappeared. It was a reply from Kathryn, 'Yes I certainly would like to be kept up-to-date, when and where do you have in mind ?'

Jim let the answer flow from his mind

'This evening, seven o'clock, the Mexican restaurant on the high street in South Croydon, the one with the bright frontage in the shadow of the refurbed tower block ?'

"Know it, see you at seven'

The Man witnessed the exchange, "excellent" he commented, "now I will go get my girl from school, if all's good I'll head back to the shop check all's okay whilst I strongly suggest you get yourself prepped and smelling sweetly for your evening, hey, get our name in the papers."

The two men rose, slapped palm against palm, gripped their hands, pulled each other closer and with a mutual slap on the back parted ways, The Man exited the flat. Jim in smiling contentment surveyed his abode, right he thought, 'do I even have a shirt that doesn't smell of weed ?' Jim got cleaning.

There are more than one refurbished tower blocks on the high street in south Croydon, and they shelter a number of Mexican restaurants and bright frontage did apply to many of them. Jim did have a clear picture of where he meant, Kathryn had a clear picture of where she thought he meant, it was not the same place. It was three minutes past seven o'clock when Kathryn called Jim. They quickly established they were not at the same place, "okay" declared Jim, "I am looking at two large bright red chilis." "So am I" concurred Kathryn. "Okay, do they have sombreros on ?" continued Jim. "No, no they do not" replied Kathryn. "Ah hah" responded Jim, "so what are they wearing ?" "This maybe a little easier" replied Kathryn patiently if I simply text you the name of the restaurant I'm standing outside of.." "That it might." Concurred Jim finishing the call with a smile. His phone beeped a moment and within five minutes he was approaching Kathryn who was stood outside the restaurant. Jim smiled sheepishly and took a glance at the big red chilis dancing in the window, they were wearing gunbelts.

Jim followed Kathryn inside, only three of thirty odd tables was occupied, a member of staff standing in the far corner indicated for them to sit wherever they liked, Kathryn selected a table in an elevated section of the room at the spot the furthest possible distance from any other diners. That spot was in a corner of wall and window. Kathryn took the benchseat that backed on to the wall leaving to Jim take the opposite chair, which proved rather rickety so he swiftly swapped it for a chair at the next table. The waitress signed that she would bring over starters, to which both Jim and Kathryn replied with a thumbs up.

"So" began Kathryn "when we last sat down Sunday all was going swimmingly, since then, there's been an attempt to ram raid you, the council have shut you down, then mysteriously quickly allowed you to reopen again so yes "a source close to the organisation" what gives ? "

"Well if a week's a long time in politics half a week's a bloody long time in shopkeeping."

Kathryn laughed, “well it makes no difference to the story, the paper went to bed tonight, and we didn’t use any of it, we couldn’t be sure of anything, what could we say ? The UK’s first legal retailer of marijuana has opened its’ doors to great excitement, queues down the street, first week of trading done, Monday night of the second week gets ram raided, Tuesday morning closed by order of the council, Tuesday afternoon reopened by order of the council.. Why ? We have no idea and people do still rely on print journalists to get in right you know, so we just went with ‘amazing opening week’ “peace man the drugs war is over” says a source close to and ‘no comment from the police’ as yet, we couldn’t get one, so pretty much all stuff you Mr Shopkeeper would like to see right, so the presses are now rolling and that cannot be changed, now you tell me what’s really gone on.”

Kathryn fixed Jim with a stare so intense it went straight through him, out through the window and into the street, outside catching the eye of a passing pedestrian.

“Right” began Jim, “so firstly you do already have a pretty clear timeline of events. Though and also there have been other events too, of which you are not aware, and which have indeed led me to arranging this meal this evening, but we can come to that later, but of the events I think that you’re aware of yes they pretty did much happen in the order you describe them.”

They were interrupted by the waitress bringing over a plate of quesadillas, taquitos and nachos, she delivered the plate and accompanying water jug with the widest of smiles whilst cheerfully recanting, “let me know when you’re ready to order your main” before sashaying back to her far corner of the restaurant.

“Okay” said Kathryn giving her delayed response, “so how come the council opened you back up again so quickly ? No wait, start at the beginning, Sunday night, we ate Lebanese, Monday morning you went to work..”

“Monday evening” continued Jim adding a topping to a Nacho, “after the shop had closed the guys from the CLA, the cannabis licensing authority came round and installed that second till I was talking about, and then when I was locking up after that wham bam some beep drove a stolen BMW X5 right at the shop crashing into the bollards while I was standing right there !”

Kathryn's jaw dropped.

"Yeah I know, it really happened," lamented Jim consoling himself with a few bites of mexican food, which did provide him some solace.

"I saw the car being taken away, " confirmed Kathryn, "I've not heard of any arrests."

"Well the police can't be trying that hard cause this is a bloke that does leave DNA."

"Eh ?"

"It turns out the car was being driven by Big Dom."

"Big Dom ?"

"I've met him, he came to say sorry."

"Oh that's nice"

"Mmm, isn't it, so it turned out he was a mate of a street dealer who was an associate of one of my members of staff.. and... and well he's promised not to do it again."

Kathryn giggled.

Jim continued, "anyway the following morning the gentleman from Croydon council decided it was unsafe to have stolen cars driven at the spot where our customers stand, which to be fair it really isn't, and yes Tuesday morning he did declare us closed."

"Yet Tuesday afternoon you were open ?"

"He used the wrong law."

"He used the wrong law ?"

"Exactly that, he used the wrong law to close us down, and so we were able to open up again ?"

"And how did you know he used the wrong law ?"

"That is a very good question."

"So how did you know he used the wrong law ?"

"Somebody told me."

"Who ?"

"Oh dear that's the thing with publicity isn't it , not everybody wants it, the person who told me the law was wrong doesn't want people to know that the wrong law was used publically, whereas what I want, what I would like, please, is as much publicity for the shop as possible. You see following Big Dom's failed attempt at a ram raid the other night a few more criminal elements have taken an interest in Legal Jims. You've seen my security guys right, Matt and Simon, big chaps right, well this morning this huge guy a foot taller than either of them just came and stood across the street watching us for half an hour, when my business associate approached himself he said he was member of a cartel and either half the business goes to him on the shop burns down. Well myself and my business associates figure the best way we can protect ourselves from being burnt down is with a blaze of publicity."

Jim stopped talking, Kathryn looked at him with a mildly reduced stare.

"So you want my help in preventing yourself and your legitimate drug dealing associates to being taken over by another gang of illegitimate drug dealers ?..."

Her words hang in the air.

Jim did not smile sheepishly nor did he laugh, her query carried a weight which that made that seem inappropriate.

"Listen Jim, I believe I made my position clear but evidently not clear enough. I think smoking is bad because it is the biggest single identifiable cause of death in this country. It kills the most people. It is bad for you, and it smells rank."

"Also the smoking of marijuana is worse because it causes damage to your mental health, removes your desire to achieve anything and up until two weeks ago was, quite rightly I think, illegal in this country."

"Yet here you are asking me to help you promote it ? Jim..."

"Wait, please wait," demanded Jim with as much gravitas as he could muster, "I certainly understand your position, I do, but will you at least hear the counter argument ?"

Kathryn sat back, the waitress waved a menu from across the room, Kathryn politely held up her hands in a waiting gesture and addressed Jim, "Okay I will."

"So have you heard of the rule of thirty-five ?"

"The rule of thirty-five ?"

"Yes."

"No I have not."

"Not surprised, they don't publish it much, it says that if you quit smoking before the age of thirty-five there aren't actually any long term deficits to your health. They don't publicise it because every young person would just start smoking with gay abandon okay, but actually they can. Yes all right unregulated smoking is too much, but managed smoking, well that there is a boon to life. And I still reach for the absolute fact of an argument that reaching for a smoke is a damn sight better than reaching for a knife, gun, bomb or freakin' prayer book."

Kathryn stared at him in cold contemplation.

"Do I have to make the artistic argument which pretty much begins with sergeant peppers lonely hearts club band and goes on from there, good smoke makes for good music, and it so ingrained the art forms and histories of other cultures. I would like sit a smoky bar while a smokin' blues player is reeling out their song."

"Sounds awful, I wouldn't be anywhere near the place."

Jim laughed.

"And your second argument that smoking marijuana is bad for your mental health, well yes it is if you are aged fourteen and nineteen, I concur, it really really is, and well what do you think happens right now ? Can fourteen to nineteen years old get hold of marijuana, of unregulated strength and effect, yes, of course they can, can they get it from me, no, no they can't, regulation of marijuana protects kids, and you know who sells to kids, Big Dom who drove the car at me, of and by the way the thing about removing all ambition…"

"Yes ?"

"Well you know you might well have a point about that.. ..up until a few weeks ago."

Kathryn smiled not an approving smile, but a semi-understanding smirk, she waved heartily at the waitress in the corner who skipped across the room with the menus and began removing the starters, Kathryn and Jim's eyes eagerly scanned the selection. Looking up Kathryn saw the waitress make a button pressing motion and looking down she realised there was a keypad set into the table from which their order could be placed. Looking up she saw the waitress was already aware of her discovery. Kathryn and Jim continued selecting. While their faces were occupied with the activity Kathryn idly spoke.

"So you yourself were a stoned shop worker for much of your life, and then the government changed the law, you took the opportunity, and now you're an entrepreneur, is that fair ?"

"I suppose so" Jim idly replied.

"So if the opportunity hadn't come along, you would still be a stoned shop worker.."

"Well a… well a… well I guess we'll never know."

"Well what else might you have done ?"

"I don't know but yes, if you must know, my lack of ambition did bug me, very much so but no I do not know what I might have done."

"Mmm" replied Kathryn contemplatively, "you know, mind if I choose, I've seen two sharing dishes that really compliment each other."

"Go right ahead."

Kathryn started typing carefully and precisely into the keyboard. Jim watched her, only when she was complete did Jim then begin to speak.

"Do you know the earliest recorded use of marijuana was in history ?"

"Nope"

"It was burnt at Chinese funerals to ease the suffering of grief."

"Is that so ?"

"That is so, traces of marijuana at this cemetery in the pa.. in some mountains near a plateau."

"Okay."

"So the earliest recorded use is to ease the pain of grief. Its' use is inscribed in ancient religious practices and it simply has been part of human existence for as long, as I dunno, cats and dogs.

"And.."

"Well it's only been recently in the six odd thousand years of recorded history that marijuana has been banned, demonised, made to appear like a disease and out-lawed, when it's basically nature's glorious free way of making us feel good. You say there's a threat to people's mental health from marijuana, I say life is a threat to people's mental health and marijuana is there to help."

Jim stopped. He could go no further. He knew he had said what he wanted to say and to go on would spoil it. He knew deep inside he wanted Kathryn to like him, and he wanted her to be accepting of his ethos, however it was clear smoking was an anathema to her, Jim could not find a reason to resume speaking. The main course arrived and Kathryn directed the waitress as to which plate went where. Once the commotion of the delivery had died down Kathryn looked at Jim, splayed her fingers wide and invited him to tuck in, Jim managed a sheepish smile, and as he reached for a first morsel Kathryn spoke up.

"I used to drink you know."

Jim, who did not know, looked at her calmly and blankly.

"There were issues and I used to drink to make myself feel good. The end result was that I did not feel good and I lost my driving licence, my livelihood and some good friends. I was stupid and I take responsibility, now, but what I do not do is go around making a living encouraging other people to drink."

Jim hadn't taken a bite of his first morsel, he didn't now, he closed his mouth, moved his head up and down a little and then spoke affirmatively, "well done, good on you taking control of your destiny, I'm only just finding out about that now and heck you know what.."

"..I've never even had a driving licence"

Kathryn raised her eyebrows.

“South London born and raised, never needed one, we’ve got trams.”

Jim and Kathryn tucked in, during the next break in eating Jim took the opportunity to speak.

“”Alcohol and Marijuana are different you know..”

“Are you suggesting I try getting stoned instead of getting pissed ?

“No. But Alcohol is a depressant.”

“Not the way I used it.”

“Err, well medically it’s a depressant, cannaboids are a stimulant, and yes well they can cause either euphoria or anxiety.. I guess it depends somewhat on the thoughts already within that persons mind.. and the situation they’re in.”

Kathryn had a full mouth and could not comment, Jim continued.

“What ethos-wise I want to get away from is cannabis use/marijuana use being regarded as this awful addiction that befalls the afflicted and the lost in the society, and see it treated more as a route to new and improved ways of thinking, it really does open up neural pathways you know, I mean the people thousands of years ago reckoned they were communicating with their god, I mean like, you know that’s not my bag, but if you go into a good smoke with positive vibes and good energy, you never know where you can go.”

Kathryn had now completely finished her chewing.

“And if you go in with negative vibes, there’s no limit to how low you can go.”

Jim took a very large mouthful.

“Which was my experience, no the ‘ol ganja has never sat right with me, not my poison, alcohol is just a little simpler and a little more available.”

“Until now.”

“Until now. So what do you think we are likely to see now, well say in the next six months, you doing good business doesn’t seem to be in doubt, but in society, in Croydon society, an increase in opiate addiction ? A general lethargy overtake the people as the local populous succumbs to becoming lotus eaters ?”

"The lotus eaters lived in a state of perpetual bliss."

Kate contemplated the comment as she took a small bite, consumed it swiftly and continued.

"My worry is this, that this genuinely will cause an increase in withdrawls in trauma and in mental breakdowns, only we won't see it happening until it's too late, it'll only become noticeable in six months when the bins aren't collected, there's no-one to open the shops, no-one to tend to the children or the elderly because everyone's bloomin' stoned !

"Well well well I take your prediction of doom and gloom and I refute it, I refute it as clearly as I possibly can ! I see a future community of happy smiling faces, of people at peace with themselves and because of that at peace with the people around them."

"Dude this is Croydon !"

A laugh burst from within Jim, unfortunately it took with it the food particles from his teeth, fortunately he was facing away from Kathryn at the time, though there was much dabbing with a napkin necessary before Jim could resume conversing.

"You know what I think, I think the people who want to see only doom and gloom because of the existence of my little shop will only see doom and gloom, and the people, the people who are open-minded to possibility well they, they might see quite wonderful things, what I'd like if there was truly a way of measuring whether or not my legally selling marijuana was actually good or bad for people ? A genuine methodical test let's say taken now, and taken in six months as to if society has improved or deproved ?

"Deproved ?" questioned Kathryn.

"You get what I mean, I don't know, you could use crime figures, the happiness index, house prices, whatever, and I really do think you'll see an improvement because of shops like Legal Jims. Though I know instead what we'll probably see is doom sayers and right wing pundits declaring it a disaster whatever the actual practical effect."

"I'm not changing Jim, I don't like smoking, but I can see your point, and yes I'm into the truth of things and if there was a true way to measure the effect of the existence of your little business this would be the time to take some readings and then see what changes, and you know what, let's do that, I get the crime figures at the paper, I can take a financial snapshot of the current rates and rents round your gaff, and it's really not that hard to find out the numbers of hospital admissions and mental health sectionings, I'll do the digging and tell you what, half a year from now let's see whether or not Croydon is winning or loosing with regards to your little business."

"Good." Declared Jim. "And thank you, that's all I ask, a fair and honest assessment of the effect of my doing business."

"And if it proves that your affect is negative will you close.."

Jim did not have an answer. He made some muttering noises as they cleared up their table, he had already noticed the keypad included a cardswipe, so as he moved to insert his plastic he suggested, "donation to charity ?"

Kathryn did not approve. She waved her goodbyes to the waitress and they headed for the door, it had started to rain slightly so they said their goodbyes in the foyer, Kathryn spoke first, "we will most likely run another piece on you in the next issue, as long as the queues continue, and I will try and an assess.. " She thought about her words, "a measurable picture of Croydon as it is now."

"Brilliant" said Jim as he tried to think of some pithy parting words, his brain wanted to say, 'and good luck with drinking', his mind stopped it and inserted, " thanks so much for your company and I'll be really intrigued with what you find out."

Jim held the door open and Kathryn darted away into the night.

VIII. Saturday night

Day eleven. The morning meeting. Six men stood wearing the brown coat of Legal Jims. Two men wore black suits. The eight formed a natural octagon, there was nothing said, there was no need to speak, everyone knew their jobs, everyone had been doing their jobs. One spliff went round from left to right, the other from right to left, the meeting was brought to a close with nods and Legal Jims opened for trading.

As the day got going Jim slipped around the shop having a quiet words with each staff member and around ten o'clock slid into the back room swapped his brown coat for a jacket and mentioned to The Man, "right I'm off to the bank, gonna set up the system that pays Rob, Anthony, Paul and Zeke, and the tax contributions and national insurance contributions on their behalf, time to pay the costs of being legit. I've spoken to Matthew and Simon, they're on board, how's it work with them, you pay them, the security company pays them, we pay them ?"

"Security's always cash, but make it so we pay them, so as we can add a little more."

Jim nodded in full agreement, "and you and the growers man, how's that going to work ?"

The Man thought for a moment, "well it's still that thing, we're legal, they're not, so best keep it cash, listen I will keep the amount constant so set up a standing order from the Legal Jim account to mine and I will distribute cash to the growers."

Jim hesitated, "well in which case Man, I'm going to have to know your name.."

The Man looked Jim full in the face, "well you have known me some years now Jim, what do you think it is ?"

"Well er to me you are The Man you know, simply The Man. I've heard people call you Donny and some people call you Johnny but erm….." Jim shrugged, The Man enjoyed his expression of a cluelessness for a few moments then spoke with a twinkle in his eye and a spark in his voice.

"You were right the first time."

Eyebrows.

"I am Donald, and I'm a Donald J, I am Donald Jonathon Tetherington."

Jim wrote the name down on the list with the staff's bank details then put down the clipboard and raised his hand and initiated a warm hand shake with The Man, "Please to meet you Donald, I'm James, and now that we have been properly introduced please may I have access to your bank account."

The Man laughed and reached for his wallet.

With all the information gathered Jim made his way to the bank. As had been arranged there was a bank official waiting who knew Jim's name and showed him to a private office. Jim noted the man was fairly young, thin, and wearing a shirt and tie combination that looked like it had been chosen by somebody else. Nervously the young man beckoned for Jim to sit and then he started jabbing at his keyboard until he had the Legal Jim account information in front of him.

Jim and the nervous young banker set up the payments to Rob, Anthony, Paul, Zeke, Matthew, Simon and Donald. And inquired the banker tentatively, "what about payments to yourself ?" "Mmm, well a normal wage will suffice, wait hold on, I'll have to cover my whole rent from next month," and Jim duly selected a wage sufficient to cover his expenses. Payments all set up Jim, rose to leave, "oh well do you mind if I just ask.." blurted out the banker, then stopped. "Please do just ask," said Jim patiently. "Since you are the Jim of Legal Jims I was just wondering..?"

"Are you old enough ?" Demanded Jim.

"Twenty-one last birthday," stuttered the banker.

"In which case if you do wish to purchase marijuana there is no need to ask me subtlety, there's no need to act in an underhand way, just come into the shop and purchase it."

"I can just do that."

"You can just do that."

"But people will know."

"That my friend is an issue for you, and the people that you know, not for me, I'm Legal Jim."

Jim shook the banker's hand warmly and paternally, "don't worry" Jim said, "I'll see myself out" and smiling he successfully found his way out of the bank. Around midday Jim found himself walking down the road back to Legal Jims, he noticed the To Let sign on the adjoining shop to his being taken down. On the other side of his premises the woman who ran the laundrette was attempting to shoo Jim's queueing customers away from her door, then one of them offered her a fag so she stopped and had a smoke with them. The owner of the takeaway was standing at the door of his shop trying to woo Jim's customers inside, he gave Jim a cheerful wave, Jim slipped back into his shop as pleased as punch. As he brought his smile inside the shop, he saw staff and customers in the shop look his way and they all caught it, he needed to give a reason for his smile, so he added two thumbs up and called out, "Hey everyone's going to get paid !" The staff all cheered and the customers freely cheered the staff.

The warm vibe continued throughout the day, the shop was shut promptly at five, with all staff members keeping a firm eye on the surroundings as the back door was bolted and the shutters padlocked down. Following a series of first bumps, back slaps and hugs the men went their separate ways. Jim's route took him back to his empty flat and his couch, he fell back in the couch with one most profound feelings of satisfaction that he could ever remember, and hunger. Though he didn't dare go out for food, he might trip or fall, or the food might be off or there could be hassle in the takeaway and Jim could simply not risk anything happening that might act to spoil this absolutely perfect day. He didn't even dare turn on the TV for fear he might see something that upset him and ruin this vibe. Jim just sat and smiled. He felt a review coming on, but his brain had already completed it without he needing to add another thought. Twelve days of business complete, responsibilities taken care of, dangers anticipated and somewhere upwards of thirty thousand of his customers were sat in their homes relaxing into a really enjoyable good quality smoke. Jim felt the only decent thing he could do would be to join them. The paper leapt into his hand, the tobacco bedded itself down and the grinder swirled, his tongue darted it out in precise fashion, his fingers twiddled and finally his lighter went click.

Day twelve of trading and it was a Friday, the morning meeting formed, six brown coats, two black jackets, three spliffs containing herbs from locations across the globes began circulating, everyone was wearing sunglasses. With everyone looking gangster Jim felt he could only begin the meeting one way, "any word from the cartel ?"

"No everything's been quiet," replied the man called Donald.

"And our social media presence ?" asked Jim.

Anthony spoke up. "We are on snapchat, we got tiktoks going viral, we is chatting on Wechat, we is pinned on pinterest and got a thread on reddit. Haven't made use of Linkedin."

The older members of staff nodded approvingly, "excellent," commented Jim, "here's a hoping a blaze of publicity," he stopped talking to toke, "keeps the gangsters away."

Jim did not receive any approving nods for his comment.

Matthew spoke. "You know the bollards outside could go with repair, I've been standing outside quite a lot and that damage is really quite unsightly."

"I will get on that right away," replied Jim.

Simon spoke up, " My girl would love to make a return visit, she's not really into the smoking but she does love the spotlight and you know.."

Jim grinned, "well we've no such thing as a quiet day but how about you bring her in on Sunday and we can all make a fuss ushering her to the front of the queue."

The men nodded their understanding approval.

"Ah gee thanks guys," Simon mumbled in reply.

"Err" said Rob.

"Mmm," eyebrowed Jim.

"Pub tonight"

"Pub tonight."

Friday brought its' own natural feel good feeling to the warm vibe of Legal Jims. People were there to score and score without guilt, tension or pressure, what had been a frenetic, frequently chaotic and often unreliable transaction for so many of the customers, that is the purchasing of marijuana, had now become joyful, safe and full of so many more choices. Some folks were overawed by what was now on offer, and even in the relaxed atmosphere of Legal Jims they were still furtive about buying cannabis, slapping their hands down to conceal their purchase and then quickly sneaking it into their pocket. Other folks got inside the store, stopped, stood, and just smiled at what they saw, no-one minded, other customers simply filed past them. The schmoke shop is relaxed thought Jim as he nodded approvingly.

Clink.

"If you'd told me twelve days ago that this is where we would be at, I'd have taken that."

"Aye touch wood it's going well, I'll tell you what Paul, Tony and Zeke are great lads, they know their stuff, they work quickly, and they are just all top blokes."

"I know right, all these business worried about can they find good staff in the local area, and will you look at that, Croydon's provided three well trained drug dealers right off the bat."

Clink.

"Matthew and Simon are sound as."

Clink.

"And The Man is able to keep going with the supply ?"

"Donald you mean.."

Rob spat his drink out.

"The Man is.. is.. a Donald."

"The Man is Donald."

"Shall we stick with The Man."

"Lets"

Clink.

"So you have a dilemma ?"

"Mm hm"

"And it's not related to the shop."

"Well no, well in a way, I mean the shop, touch wood, so far, is a success right, oh and that is nice mate.."

Clink.

"I mean it is nice to be part of something successful too bloody right and I think that success must be showing a little right, cos you know I've been going around feeling good."

"Well that's bloody good right mate.." affirmed Jim, slightly hesitantly.

"Oh it is, it is, it is," confirmed Rob, "it is and it's only she has noticed.."

"The wife.."

"Yeah the wife's who spent a year living apart, doing her own thing while deciding on the divorce, well she's started taking an interest again.."

"Mmmmm"

"Mmmmm indeed, so the dilemma is, am I like ooo ooo she loves me again or am I like now hold on cos if you like really didn't love me until now.."

"Aaah"

"Well come on Jim you've met her, you know her a bit, come on in with an opinion."

"No fucking way. This is your thing, or like, a yours and hers thing all the way. Yes I've met her yes but I do not know your wife, the only thing I know is how you talk about her, and well you've talked about her like that for years, you're besotted man, you know that, so anyway that's what I know."

"Yeah well, is besotted love ?"

"Dunno, they're spelt differently."

"They are that."

Clink.

Silence settled between the men for a while.

When he was ready Rob spoke.

"I think what I want is choice, like the customers in our shop I want to be able to see a great range of possibilities in front of me.

"Ah hah," countered Jim, "but when choosing which weed, the weed you haven't chosen doesn't get pissed off and leave."

"Yes but how do you know the weed you haven't chosen is good weed anyway ?"

"By marrying it for a year first… you know what this isn't really working as an analogy."

"True that."

" So, if talking really now, since you have already been married for a year you must kinda know."

"I guess."

"Well why exactly were you breaking up ?"

"I dunno, I guess I wasn't trying hard enough.."

"And well would you try hard enough another time around ?"

"I guess."

"And does she make you want to be a better man ?"

"She wants me to already be a better man, then she'll come in and take over."

Clink.

"Like it is" spoke Rob and Jim simultaneously.

After the due period Rob piped up with something new, " so where do you see the business going ?"

"Well I was having this conversation with The Man yesterday. He sees a chain of shops, I must admit I don't see it the same way, it's the worry of becoming the British East India Company."

"Yes it's a common fear."

"Exactly. Dope is beautiful man, to those that appreciate it. I don't wanna force no dope on no-one that doesn't want it. They have their thing, we'll have our thing, it's all cool, but become big, get sales targets you have to hit or else, and well it'll just take the love out of it."

"Could be a missed opportunity, we got a lot of eyeballs pointing our way right now, the authorities and that, well at this moment they should just nod through whatever we want to do, this could be the moment."

"You'd be a big factor in that, are you happy to be the sole on site shop manager while the Man and I go setting up other shops ? Heck do I even want to go setting up other shops, I like our shop, might even go as far as saying I love our little shop."

"Steady on."

"Well just maybe and going with the tried and tested if it ain't broken don't fix it method and I am content to simply shopkeep in our little shop, I did fifteen years in the Jewellery store quite happily."

"You were bored, frustrated and unhappy with yourself all the time."

"Yeah well this is England, that's what passes for quite happily."

"So now you're saying you're quite content to now do another fifteen years in another store."

"Yes, though with a share of the profits in this one, and you know, name above the door 'n all that, plus it's a product that I'm personally fairly keen on."

Clink.

"There is that, so you know that's kinda helped me decide. You see if you, faced with the chance at greater riches than you have, aren't really that keen on the idea, well that sort of points me in a certain direction.."

"Does it now ?"

"That it most certainly does, another pint ?"

"Definitely."

At four pints each Jim and Rob called it a night, they hugged and headed their separate ways, Jim to his home and Rob to the Kebab shop beneath his flat. As he stood there waiting patiently for his large chicken sheesh to be prepared he heard the sound of copious vomiting on the street outside, he did not turn around, no longer my problem he smiled to himself.

Jim arrived back to his flat, mildly bruised and battered from a drunken stumble, but otherwise unharmed. No point in topping off the drink with a spliff he sensibly thought and he did remember to drink a pint of water to ward off a hangover before collapsing into bed. His sleep was disturbed by having to get up three times to pee.

Day thirteen of trading at Legal Jims commenced without Jim or Rob. Donald, Paul, Tony and Zeke had the shop open on, time Matthew and Simon were on the street by nine fifteen martialling the queue, Jim and Rob made it by nine thirty. Running in they both smiled sheepishly, as recompense each immediately took up position behind a till relieving Paul and Zeke. The first customer to approach Jim was a young woman, clean looking thought Jim, not the type of lady you would imagine being a smoker.

"Good Morning, " she cheerfully chirruped."

"Good Morning," responded Jim.

"Now I'm not normally a smoker, but I was just sitting there looking through colour swatches this morning, and well they do say marijuana is great for your colour perception, and I do bake, and seeing as I'm your number one customer."

"You're our number one customer ?" queried Jim.

"Oh you'll see" declared the lady wiggling her figure, "so for something to… to stir the way I see colour, what do you recommend ?"

"Well if you're new to the herb let's go with something low in THC, I know how about a little cherry wine ?"

"Then I'll have seven point zero eight seven grams of that please" asked the lady, wiggling her finger once more. Jim went off to prepare the order mildly perplexed but soon returned with a sealed baggie of quarter ounce of cherry wine."

He flipped over the bag, the lady slid her finger into place, Jim took in the details on the screen and raised his right eyebrow in surprise.

"You are customer number one !" He blurted.

"I am," the lady smiled, "I was working at the CLA when they were setting your machine up and they used me as their test customer, and well I thought since marijuana has been in the news so much lately, and as I'm already registered, I may as well, you, know, try it out."

"Oh well do let me know how it goes," smiled Jim warmly, "it's about twenty-five minutes to bake a good cookie and you really can add any flavours you like, never quite sure how long it takes to ingest but you should start to feel something within an hour or two."

"Thank you," chirped the lady, "I'll be most sure to bake responsibly."

"Enjoy the colour choices."

The lady left the shop, Jim looked in awe for a moment at the customer screen displaying zero zero zero zero one shaking his head in disbelief, the next customer required registration , they were customer number thirty four thousand five hundred and sixty seven. 'Funny how the numbers go," thought Jim.

Outside the shop Matthew and Simon did their thing. In a speech now very familiar to him Matthew addressed the queue, "Hi everyone thanks for waiting patiently now please listen, if you under twenty-one please just don't bother, go home now and find something more productive to do, if you have a fake ID it will not work here, we have connections and we check everyone." Two small groups of people peevishly left the queue. Matthew held up his hands for silence to prevent any jeers and cat calls, "happens everyday folks," he nonchalantly stated. Simon at the far end of the queue used his body language to echo Matthew's words, and many of those in the queue shrugged their understanding.

The smooth running of the queue was violently disturbed mid-morning with the arrival of one very bombastic man and three silently aggressively men in two flatbed trucks. Mr Bombastic leapt out the lead vehicle first, he looked at Matthew, he looked at Simon, he addressed the bollards, "Oh my poor babies what have they done to you !?" He screamed and dropped to his knees and wept. "My poor children," he continued, "you were so young and new and freshly cast, and now, just look at you now." "Why god why !?" The council repair man screamed to the heavens.

Within the store the commotion caught Jim's eye and he dashed out to the street to where the man was kneeling. Mr Bombastic tearfully got to his feet and prepared to cast further lamentations towards heaven and earth, Jim silenced him instantly with the depth of his look.

The man's lip quivered, he awaited Jim's words for if they did not delay him he was going to commence on one of the most insane sermons of his life on the fate that can befall innocents bollards.

"Sir." Said Jim,

The man waited, his lip waited.

"Sir," repeated Jim. "Your magnificent bollards saved my pitiful life. They were brilliant ! They were proud, they held fast, they held fast against the body of a BMW X5 that was being driven straight at me, and like the bravest of soldiers they faced that threat and they cast it aside, they flung that damn car into the air and skewered it. These Sir, are the best bloody bollards that have ever existed !"

By now there were tears in Jim's eyes, there were tears in the eyes of Mr Bombastic and tears beginning to well in the eyes of many of the crowd. Mr Bombastic and Jim hugged, they grasped each other and squeezed each other in pure celebration of life and bollards, people were gazing upon the scarred bollards with wonder, some tentatively reaching out to them and providing comfort, Matthew bowed his head.

"Please," said Jim breaking away from the embrace and addressing all present, "please give this man all the co-operation you can, he is doing vital work."

Jim stepped back and saluted the foreman of the bollard repair crew and he saluted right back, Jim retreated back into the store Mr Bombastic addressed his crew.

"Right I want a two metre cone perimeter around these babies, I want some pre-stressed and some high density and some rebar ready to go and available, I don't know where we're going to go with this yet, you, get started with the wire brushes, crimped brush not raw, got to be gentle with these beauties they've been through a lot, you have sandpaper standing by, not the forty stuff, gotta be sensitive, go fine, go one twenty, I want a repair cone ready to go over each bollard just in case, tight fit, zero clearance at the base and I want it now and will somebody get the bloody mixer on !"

The three surly men grudgingly moved into action, firstly the two metre perimeter was secured, all three men were involved, they moved to stand in a in circular formation around their foreman who was crouched at the bollards. Then the surly man nearest the track grabbed nine orange cones, expertly flipped three off the top and passed six to the second surly man, he too deftly removed three from the top and passed on the remaining three and with the three man each laying out three cones between them the perimeter was secured.

Matthew and Simon managed the queue on the pavement indicating quite clearly the authority of the cones.

The surly man by the truck passed out crimped wire brushes to his colleagues and laid one hand on the mixer, he gripped the rim with steely fingers and turned to his foreman, "what'll it be boss ?" he growled.

The foreman was examining the bollards in an intensive triage assessment, he felt the cracks on each one, he ran his fingers up the scars left by the car's bumper calculating the length and depth of each one, he placed his hands around the base of each bollard in turn finally placing his ear against the bollard which had suffered the most damage. Slowly he stood.

"Okay here's how it goes, these boys have been hit fast and they've been hit hard, but they took it and they took it well god bless 'em, now if they've been made to wobble and they is loose then it's pneumatic them out, full on mix and reset, however if they do not wobble then they is fine because we did our job right the first time and we can just slap a bit of postcrete on them cracks. So if they wobble, we're here for the next six hours on a Saturday, if they don't wobble, we're done in ten minutes. Understood ?"

The surly men nodded.

The previously bombastic foreman nervously took hold of the first bollard, the workers watched with baited breath, he grasped the concrete protrusion, held fast and shook for all his might. The bollard held, the workers sighed.

The foreman moved slowly and steadily to the second bollard took it in both hands, looked up at his watching crew, secured his grasp and once more attempted a mighty shake. The bollard did not budge, the workers cheered.

The foreman wiped sweat from his brow with the back of his hand and then slowly and surely addressed the third bollard. He eyed it up and down first, looking for some hint of how it might react to his shaking, the bollard gave nothing away. The foreman grabbed it in throttling position, he squeezed his hands and he shook and he shook and tried all he could to force it away from him then pull it to his chest. Not a millimetre of movement, not one iota of concrete dust was released, the workers cheered, the watching crowd cheered, Simon punched the air in glee.

The foreman addressed the final bollard, this time there was no eyeing up first , he was straight down on his haunches hands around the cylinder and he clenched. He held position for a moment, the crowd gasped, one of the surly men removed his hard hat, another coughed. The foreman shook. His flesh across his body rippled, he pushed forward, he pulled backwards, the bollard did not move.

The crowd broke into rapturous applause, Simon began the chant "bollards bollards bollards", it wasn't taken up. The foreman arose and addressed his men, "right forget that fucking mixer, chuck me a bag of postcrete and we'll be fucking done in five minutes."

The surly man by the truck grabbed a ten kilo plastic bag from the back of the flatbed and hurled it at his foreman who caught it stomach first.

"Right ,"said the foreman to his workers, "I got this, anyone who wants to fucking shop here can, whatever."

With that the foreman dove his hand into the plastic bag and began scooping out a grey goo which he shovelled into the cracks, all the surly men joined the queue for Legal Jims. Matthew and Simon both took up position nearby in support of the cones.

The foreman upped his game moving swiftly from bollard scooping up the goo, slapping it in the cracks with the front of his hand and smoothing it down with the back, within a few minutes every crack had been filled and casually and ineptly smoothed down. The foreman knew this, he was the foreman for a reason, resentful at now having to correct his own work he walked out of the cone circle and to the back of the truck to collect the sandpaper, ensuring his queueing workers were aware of his utter annoyance at having to do such a thing himself. He returned to silent solemnity of the sacred cone circle and knelt at the first bollard, breathing heavily upon the goo to hasten the drying process pressing and prodding each part he blew on assessing whether or not it was ready to receive some vigorous sand papering. As he proceeded with his task the foreman soon dismissed with any such assessments, assumed the goo was set and just sandpapered the lot.

Most eyes were soon cast aside from the foreman and his work but from within the shop Jim remained transfixed. He knew that on a scale which ran from being destitute and without hope, to being content and secure, his life did now rank on the upper range of that scale, and he also knew that he would not be there if it were not for those mighty bollards that Mr Bombastic was now repairing so badly. Jim closed his eyes in silent contemplation of the mighty act they had performed. He notice the three surly workmen were reaching the front of the queue and quickly pushed Zeke away from behind the till and took up position.

The first surly man approached, grumbled his order, Jim took his finger, gave it a clean, performed the registration duties, prepared the order and handed it to the man, then when the moment came to pay Jim held out his palm in rejection of the surly man's offer of a card, the man halted, and Jim produced his own card and made the payment himself, "Tell your boss thank you" Jim said. The surly man hadn't been planning to say anything when he made his purchase and now he didn't know what to say, so he just spat on the counter and moved off.

The second surly man approached the counter, grunted his order, Jim applied the wet wipes to his finger, conducted the processes and once more at the moment of payment Jim denied the surly man's advances and proffered his own card to pay. The second surly man nodded his understanding and turned his face almost ten degrees to the left to acknowledge he had first conversation, Jim acknowledged his slight facial movement with a barely perceptible head dip.

As the second surly man slouch off the third and final surly man approached the counter, he glared at Jim resentfully. “Acapulco Gold if you don’t mind” he hissed, Jim touched the wet wipes towards him as he went to the gold form the drawer. The surly man ignored the wet wipes. Jim let it go, indicated how the registration system went, the man, complied, then Jim wiped the screen afterwards. With registration and sale complete the third surly man did not reach for his wallet though once more Jim did reach for his, and as he made the payment Jim again uttered, “Tell your boss thank you.” The man glared accusingly at Jim in response, his eyes brimming with aggression. “I’ll tell him,” he sneered.

Jim took one step back from the counter and performed the quickest of salutes, all of the surly men were uncomprehending of the act and with dark mutterings made their way out of the shop. Jim watched through the window as they made way into the cone circle and up to their boss begrudgingly showing him their purchases and it seemed to Jim that they were making vague gestures to their boss that the bloke in the shop wanted to thank him for saving his life. Mr Bombastic the council repair foreman appeared to be able to interpret and understand the gestures and he turned to face Jim through the window, rose to his full height of five foot four, and presented a full and proper, longest way up, shortest way down, salute to Jim. Jim stood to his full height and did precisely the same.

The bollard repair foreman returned to his regular activities of harassing and lambasting his crew insisting they keep their purchases well out of sight on council time and slamming sandpaper into their hands haranguing them into correcting the corrective work that he commenced on the bollards. Mr Bombastic then left the cone circle and went to stand by the truck and attempted to mirror the stances of Matthew and Simon as he oversaw events.

Jim retired to the back room for a moment, Rob spotted and followed him through to the privacy of the rear of the shop. They grinned at each other.

“Bollards saved my life,” explained Jim.

"They did a better job than I could have done," acknowledged Rob, "my body's always been useless against speeding cars."

The men laughed and hugged.

Extricating themselves Rob swiftly spoke, "So you know how it's family day tomorrow ?"

"Eh ?"

"Simon bringing his girlfriend in for a celebrity purchase."

"Oh right."

"Well I was thinking same. I was thinking I could bring the wife, and yep she is still legally my wife, in to the store so she could like, be involved in what I do, see me at work, you know, see the activity that brings the money in."

"Mmm I see it I see it, okay tomorrow's Sunday, we open at ten, howsabout we all get here for nine thirty, you can show her round the shop while it's empty master of all you purvey."

"Whoa whoa whoa there dude, morning meeting first, she can come in after ten same as the other customers."

"Word."

The two men slapped their right hand palms against each other and grasped firmly, grinned and left the back of the shop.

Saturday rolled on, the workmen completed their repair of their boss's repair. The hallowed ground of the cone circle was deconsecrated and the nine cones hurled unceremoniously onto the back of the flat beds. The Boss gave his gravest and most sombre nods to Matthew and Simon, who performed the most minor head dips possible in return, and with that the surly bollard repair team and their bombastic boss accompanied by much slamming, reslamming and slapping of van doors exited the area, begrudgingly.

Within the shop Jim now retreated into the back of the shop with The Man, speaking swiftly he relayed the conversation he had had with Rob.

“So tomorrow as family day ? Simon’s bringing his girl, Rob wants to bring in his wife. I was wondering if you wanted to bring the family in too ?”

“Jim my daughter is eight.”

“Okay so there’s that.”

“I like that you’re feeling confident, but we don’t know that the danger’s passed, we don’t know what the cartel will do next, if anything, I’ve had word from my lady, she’s on her way back, and I won’t know how it goes until I know what she knows, capiche ?”

“Err I think so, “mumbled Jim,.

“Good enough !” Winked The Man, “Now I have places to be, you got his for the rest of the day ?”

Jim nodded.

“Okay I am outta here, see you, at ten, in the morning for some family fun.”

And with a swift fist bump The Man slid out the back door of the shop. Jim returned to the front of the shop and at opportune moments quickly had a word with the family day idea with the rest of the staff, “noted” said Matthew, Paul mumbled “I don’t actually have..” “Not me, happily single, “replied Anthony, Zeke nodded his understanding of the question.

Five o’clock soon rolled up, Matthew and Simon ushered away those who had arrived too late, Jim, Rob Anthony, Paul and Zeke, gave the store the first proper brushing down it had had in first two weeks, and with no customers and seven members of staff present they felt safe enough to open the front door and back doors of the shop simultaneously and enable a current of air to sweep through the shop. As the light wind blew over the boxes it picked up all the scents of the drawers and whisked them through the doorway out into the Croydon street. Matthew and Simon and standing in the threshold received the full flavour of the magical draft, each of them breathing in the delightful odour and smiling with the utmost pleasure and satisfaction.

"Right" declared Matthew, "That's the nice bit of work over for the day, we are now going to do the nasty bit and go and stand outside the night club and deal with the alkies.

"Good luck to you and thanks lads, " stated Jim, securely locking the front door once their reassuring presence had departed.

"Paul, Anthony, Zeke, thank you see you for ten in the morning."

The youngsters skedaddled out of the back door, "Rob, pub ?"

"Can't tonight mate, it's whaddya call it, date night."

"Uh huh" Jim and Rob followed the youngsters out of the back door bolting it behind them, then having walked round to the front of the shop Rob performed look out duties as Jim brought down the shutters and padlocked them to the ground. They both inspected the repairs to the bollards, sighed, and went their separate ways. Once more Jim's route took him back to his empty flat, unsurprisingly there was no one there to greet him and no movement or sounds emanating from any of the rooms. No one was watching anything on the telly and there were no smells of cooking drifting out of the kitchen. Jim, taking in all this nothingness slumped onto the sofa and contemplated starting a conversation with the wall, his sacred box winked at him from the coffee table.

IX. The Climax

Jim slept well and contentedly though he awoke confused, he knew it was Sunday, he let everything else come into focus in its' own time. Late start at work was thought number one, there is nobody else here was thought number two, essentials established Jim got down to the fundamentals and tried to work out which room he was in. Lounge, he was in the lounge, the feel of the couch cushions against his butt confirmed that. Having established his position a plan formulated, from lounge to bathroom to kitchen, he decided to carry it out later in the day.

Jim returned to sleep. Later he awoke, he remembered the plan but realised he needed to re-evaluate it in the light of not knowing what time it was. His fumbling hands found his mobile and pressed the side buttons, the screen read zero nine zero three. "Doable" spoke Jim and threw himself off the couch and into his plan.

Shower and face slap, four minutes, juice from the carton and one slice of unbuttered bread ninety seconds, clothes, hair, brown coat three minutes, locate shop and flat keys fifteen minutes, Jim cursed the couch for always concealing with such cunning all that it consumed. Run to the tram stop, barely possible, wait for tram, six minutes and arrival in Croydon at zero nine fifty one, Jim grinned, he had the time to compose himself as he strolled from tram stop to store. He sidled around the corner of the building to join in for the morning meeting, and found it comparatively deserted. Paul was prominent and he had set up a little table and was setting about rolling the most complex of spliffs having his papers laid out in the shape of a tree, replete with roots. Zeke stood over him advising whilst Simon provided security, nodded greetings were exchanged and Simon explained. "The Man called, he'll be along later, Matthew called, he'll be along later." Zeke spoke, "Tony's picking up his mum, he'll be along later." "Okay" said Jim correlating the information, "and since Rob's wife is coming in later Rob too will be along later."

"He'll be here now," announced Rob arriving at the meeting.

"He is here now," confirmed Jim nodding in his presence.

"Right Zeke, Paul, carry on, Simon if you would do the honours on the street Rob tis you and I each with a till to ourselves, now, time to greet the worshippers !"

Jim and Rob entered the shop via the backdoor, Simon took the shop keys round the front to open the shutters. The clear air established the day before had overnight been once more infused with the aroma of marijuana strains from all over the world, all combining to produce a heady intoxicating ambience within the shop, Rob and Jim sucked it in, "Not a bad way to start the day hey", grinned Rob. On the pavement outside Simon flung the shutters upwards and the store was flooded with light painting Jim and Rob in silhouettes of dazzling sunlight and framing them as angels. Simon unlocked the door and poked his head in. "Ready to go ?" He questioned, "Yes my son replied Jim."

Simon fully opened the door and the faithful began to enter. Quietfully and respectfully they milled in slowly succumbing to awe and excitement as the realised what they were about to quite legally and as joy began to ebb into their faces Jim smiled upon them beatifically.

The first hint that the day might not go as expected came with a change in the odour. Rob was the first to notice as the flavour of the air around him changed from sweet to sour. He looked across, moments later Jim caught it too. They both glanced outside looking for its' source and saw only Simon standing outside the window sniffing the air inquisitively.

A van pulled up on the far side of the road, the drivers window was down ever so slightly but sunlight reflecting off the glass pane prevented them seeing who was inside. The rear doors of the van flung open and two trunk sized legs flew out and hit the ground with a thundering wallop. A torso came next followed by arms and a head. Initially it didn't appear as if all the parts of the body were going to cooperate however with access to the air they appeared to gain a certain synchronicity and within a few moments the fully complete figure of the man mountain was visible across the street.

Man mountain didn't look either way when crossing the street. He didn't have to, the traffic had already seen him and had already stopped. So he strolled across the street in his own time taking short steps. Immediately outside Legal Jims mountain man stumbled slightly on the kerb and put his hand out onto one of the bollards to steady himself. The bollard wobbled.

Jim was in the shop knowing he had to do something but not knowing what to do. He was expecting Simon to come flying in through the shop window at any moment, he had to do something, his body dashed to the front door, his mind voiced many objections to the action but in the end went with him. Simon pulled open the shop door and stepped out on to the street. He took up position standing shoulder to shoulder along side Simon and joined him in staring directly at the man mountain, then looking higher, then looking a little higher still until Simon was looking him directly in the eyes and then Simon panted and panted and panted.

Man mountain regarded Simon and Jim. Slowly, very slowly, his gaze moved from one to the other, assessing them, re-assessing them and no doubt deciding, thought Jim, which one of them it was practical to crush first.

Man mountain rumbled. A thought appeared to be spreading across his face and its' vocalisation was beginning its' journey from diaphragm to gullet. His face stopped moving as he focussed all his efforts on the coming words, they appeared to bounce around his adam's apple for a while before suddenly bursting forth from his humungous mouth.

"You guys !" The Man Mountain cried out !

Man mountain flung his left arm around Jim, he flung his right around Simon, and he squeezed them and he hugged them so tightly that for a few moments Simon and Jim became one.

Man mountain released Jim and Simon into their respective states of shock and as they stood there quivering they looked up at him agape and aghast and they could see that the enormous volume of man mass towering above them was crying.

"You guys !" He wailed once more and Simon and Jim braced themselves for what seemed to be a second incoming hug. Instead Man Mountain rested himself on Simon's shoulder and prepared to complete his sentence.

"Your man. The other day. What he said. Well it was right you know. And so I went back to the cartel. And they're going to open a legit shop. And I'm the front man."

Jaws dropped, realisation that neither fight nor flight was necessary spread across Simon and Jim, Rob in the shop took his hand away from dialling the third nine on his phone keypad.

Man mountain continued.

"So. For the first time in my life. I'm going to have. A proper with healthcare ! And. The cartel have arranged. My own car and driver." Man mountain indicated the van across the street and the driver's window whirred down to reveal Big Dom giving a thumbs up.

"All I wanted to do. Was to come and say. Thank you. Your man, you guys…"

Simon and Jim braced.

"You guys. Have given. Me the chance at. A better life. Thank you."

With that Man Mountain gave Simon and Jim a sheepish gleeful smile and turned to make his way back across the street. The traffic stopped, Big Dom leapt round to the back of the van to help Man Mountain to lumber in and with each delivering an enormous parting wave the two got in, the van sunk down a couple of inches and strained its' way away from Legal Jims.

Simon and Jim collapsed into relieved laughter, Rob ran outside to join them, phone still in hand, "I'd have called the cops if I had to, " he explained, "What just happened !?" He demanded. "They're opening their own shop, "replied Jim between giggles. "Opening their own shop ?" Questioned Rob, Simon nodded confirmation. "Rob while you've got your phone out, text The Man, he needs to know, tell him exactly that, 'The cartel have visited, they are opening their own shop.'" "Will do" replied Rob starting to type though still shaking his head with disbelief at the information he'd just heard.

Rob's phone beeped confirmation his text has been received and he and Jim returned to the shop to hurriedly began working through the queue that had formed while the Man Mountain had been present. As there was no queue or any other visible dangers outside of the shop Simon came in and assisted with preparing the orders, the three working together swiftly relieving the pressure at the tills. Within a few minutes the shop had been returned to what had become its' usual calm until there was another quite notable change in the air.

"She's approaching" announce Rob.

"That perfume, only her, battle stations."

It was at that moment Paul and Zeke returned from out the back of the store. It was at that moment Jim remembered that they had even been out there. From the grins on their faces and the smoke emanating from their mouths Jim deduced they had completed their construction of the arboreal spliff.

"You should try this." Declared Zeke.

"Try what ?" Inquired a demanding female voice from the shopfloor.

Heads turned.

"Absolutely nothing," announced Jim, "Rob I believe your wife is here," he said to Ron and "Guys !" he instructed Paul and Zeke approaching them with fingers clearly indicating they should be exiting the way they came in. Paul realised what was going on, Zeke did not, but both allowed themselves to be herded through the back of the shop and out through the back door. "Guys, it's just because Rob's wife's turned up at the exact same time and do remember, not on the premises."

"But boss" interjected Paul, "we're not on the premises.

It was then Jim realised that the outside meeting area had changed since that morning, it was not outside anymore. What had begun with Paul's table that morning was now covered by a fabric awning firmly supported by steel posts. Paul clicked his fingers, Zeke pulled a rope and cloth walls rolled down on three sides isolating the group from wind and prying eyes. Paul indicated his table and the ashtray that lay upon it, and in that ash tray lay the lit spliff, it was the perfect spliff. It expanded from tight at the roach to wide at the fire and a constant rate throughout its' six inch length, it smoked appealingly, the smoke rising from the burning embers lured Jim in, he sat gingerly and delicately on the chair that Paul had been using and looked at him, inquiring for permission to take a toke.

"Go ahead Boss" smiled Paul.

Jim nodded in thanks and taking both hands, one for the filter, one for the shaft, he raised the mighty reefer to his mouth, gulped in anticipation, cleared his throat, said a couple of ahhs to ensure his throat was clear, on hearing the right the tone ne knew it was then time to continue. He pressed his lips to roach, he secured an airtight seal and he sucked.

Jim that sucked that holy smoke deep deep deep into his lungs and he did not cough. He sat back on Paul's rickety chair and it held him. He exhaled the excess smoke through his nostrils and he couldn't see a damn thing, smoke swallowed his vision and for a time Jim was blind.

He didn't mind.

He held his mind in a state of tranquil anticipation and waited for it to pass. He knew it would. Things were okay and they were going to remain okay and were okayness did take a break for a while it would soon return, and Jim knew that.

"Boss ?"

Jim thought he heard a voice but decided it couldn't be important."

"Boss ?"

Same voice, more insistent tone, Jim contemplated returning to the real world in order to reply but he really was okay in his okayness.

"Boss !" This time the tone to the voice was less inquiring and more shocked. It piqued Jim's curiosity and casually he slipped out of the world of okayness and back into reality.

"Boss" repeated the voice, this time the voice added five more words, "should they be doing that ?" Jim, back in the real world and still sat in the chair identified the source of the voice as Paul and Paul as no longer being in the tent with him but inside the shop and frantically beckoning him inside. Jim followed , Paul led him to the door to the shop, they opened the door and peeked.

The meet up between Rob and his wife had clearly gone fairly well. Rob was behind the till, his wife was directly in front of him facing in his direction, her bum was oscillating gently up and down against the finger scanning machine, her legs gradually wrapping themselves around his as her arms clung to his back as they kissed passionately.

Jim stopped and Jim thought, he looked to shop floor. Every customer that was looking at Rob and his wife, every customer was, instantly looked down as they clocked Jim looking at them. Jim thought fast, at least he thought he did, though in reality all he managed was to stand still while his jaw dropped.

A thought came to him.

"Rob" he hissed.

Rob continued to kiss.

"Rob" he hissed louder.

Rob's wife began to kiss more passionately.

"Rob !" Jim hisshouted.

Rob opened his eyes. He had been lost in the moment but the moment had come back and found him and was now firmly taking back control . As passion was replaced shock on his face Jim further hisshouted, "Rob there's now a tent out back attached to the back door. Take five."

Gratitude replaced shock and Rob yanked his wife's bum away from the finger machine and pulled her into the back of the shop and out through the back door. Paul and Zeke and Jim took up their own positions behind the counter and nobody in the shop said a single word. Simon who had been observing events from outside turned back to survey the street and found himself face to face with a formidable looking lady, nearly the same height as him, and in possession of a pointedly accusing finger, which she pointed directly at Simon's face.

"You're Simon." She declared.

“Yes” said Simon, “Yes I am”

“Well done mom,” said Anthony appearing from behind her, “Hi Simon this me mum, “ he explained,” and mum this is where I work.” Simon and Anthony’s mum shook hands and Anthony ushered her inside the shop. Anthony’s mum scanned the shop. She spotted Jim, got her finger out again and marched up to him, Anthony trailed behind.

“You’re Jim.” She declared.

“Yes Mrs.... Yes I am, “ replied Jim.

“And you have employed my son”

Jim couldn’t quite work out if the sentence was meant as a statement or a question.”

“Yes I have and he is most excellent member of staff.”

“I’m glad to hear it. And you’re doing right by him and he’s doing right by you.”

Again Jim could not work out if he was being instructed or interrogated so he selected repetition as his answer, “He is doing right by me and I will do right by him” stated Jim.

“Excellent !” Cried out Anthony’s mum and with that her finger became a palm and with both palms she grasped Jim’s face and kissed him. “Now“ she said turning to her son, “you show me all them flavours you’ve been telling me about.” “Will do mom,” laughed Anthony taking her by the hand and pulling her behind the counter to show off the shop’s wares.

Jim steadied himself for what was coming next. He glanced towards the back door, then quickly looked away just in case he did see or hear anything. He looked at Anthony eagerly showing his mother the multitude of different marijuanas available and couldn’t help but smile, he watched Paul and Zeke work the tills and listened to Paul patiently explain what tetrahydrocannabinols were to a customer eager to learn. The warm feeling of things being as they should was swiftly spoiled by the sight of Simon and his girlfriend arguing. It was apparent she had turned up once more expecting queue jumping celebrity status, and there was no queue to be jumped. She seemed to be informing Simon that the joy of legally purchasing marijuana was nowhere near as important as the joy of having a lot of people witnessing her legally purchasing marijuana. Simon’s shrugs indicated there was little he could do to change the situation and his girlfriend’s exit from the scene duly followed.

Anthony's mum finished her inspection of her son's workplace and left with a cheery wave and a "be good now to Anthony" which he seemed to find extremely embarrassing. As she left she brushed shoulders with an old man entering the shop, he tipped his hat to her and said good day madam to her, she smiled and said good day sir to him. Bolstered by the exchange the elderly man hopped and skipped his way into the shop, "Anthony, Zeke, lads !" He declared. "Gentlemen" He said addressing Jim and Paul, ooh have I got a tale to tell you !" And with that the elderly gentlemen waltzed his way across the shop floor to the counter.

Jim brought his finger into things, pointing it at the man and waving it up and down until his brain once more caught up with his body.

"You're the man with the cane !"

"Quite right Sir !" Declared the old man. "And your product has done wonders for my leg pain, it's gone, I think it was a two stage thing, the smoking took away the pain so I could bear getting up and moving about, and then once I was up and bought the regular movement has brought my legs back to life !" Following the statement the elderly gentlemen demonstrated the truth in his statement by performing a slow by perfectly executed pirouette across the shop floor. The shop staff of Legal Jims exploded into applause.

Jim felt like crying, the old man's joy was infectious, and his dancing was to Jim a manifestation of his ethos, marijuana is good, marijuana is beneficial to the human condition, and right here right now was a human benefitting, Jim swore that the smile that was forming in his heart would never leave him. He spotted Simon out on the street head suddenly snap left then right, then Simon warmly hailed to whom ever was approaching from the right and then cast an even warmer hail to whoever was approaching from the left. Keen on some good vibes Jim, Paul and Zeke hastened towards the door, Anthony remained at the till excitedly explaining to a customer what his mother's favourite marijuana was.

Jim, Paul, Simon and Zeke formed a crowd and Jim was quickly aware there were three persons approaching from the right and two from the left. He looked right first. Jim had known The Man, Donald J.Tetherington, for around fifteen years. He had always liked and respected him and having worked with him for a few weeks he absolutely adored him. Jim now saw The Man is a completely new light. To Jim The Man was the Man, he was tall strong, commanding, capable of getting things done, which for so long Jim had not been, The Man was the Boss, and rightly so, he took control and quite frankly this was a man that should have control was what Jim had always thought. Now here was The Man, standing before him with a woman who could only be The Wife of The Man, a woman who had a look on her face that simply stated, "I got him. He's mine. What I say he does. This is how it is." The look was enough but the presence of The Man and The Wife's daughter peaking between their legs confirmed the identity of all those present.

The Man turned to The Wife for permission to speak, she granted it, "So the cartel are going legit ?" he called across to Jim. "That's what they say," replied Jim, "Man mountain is gonna be their Jim, he's going to be the front man." "Well he's got a lot of it" commented The Man, a look from The Wife confirmed that would be his only comment. The Wife took a long look at the shop front, she took a look at each and every member of staff finishing on Jim, she nodded, turned and with a regal swish directed her family to return back in the direction from whence they came. The Man and his daughter swivelled.

The two persons who had been approaching from the other side waited patiently. As Jim, Simon, Paul and Zeke watched in awe as The Wife led The Man away a polite cough emanated from their left hand side. Drawn by the sound all eyes turned left and were greeted by the sight of Matthew, as ever dressed in his black ensemble with his arm around the most gorgeous and striking man the staff of Legal Jims had ever laid eyes on. He had glistening brown skin, a striking nose and the most elegant cheek bones, he matched Matthew in height though was far more slender, and was adorned in a silver suit which sparkled in perfect keeping with the gleam in his eyes. The boys in brown coats were transfixed. "Hi Afonso" called Simon, "Hi Simon" replied Afonso, his voice was beautiful too.

Matthew held Afonso tight as he turned him towards the store, “And this querida is Legal Jims, this is where I work.” “Beautiful” commented Afonso, “and we can buy here ?” “We can buy here” confirmed Matthew and he proudly swept Afonso into the store. Jim, Paul and Zeke trailed in their wake, Simon remained on his own on the street outside. As Afonso, Matthew, Zeke, Jim and Paul surveyed the shop, and Matthew showed Afonso his favourite products, a few rhythmic noises could just about be heard caused by something thudding against the back door of the shop. Zeke, Paul and Jim exchanged concerned glances, Afonso raised his eyebrows. Hurriedly Paul and Zeke took off their brown coats, and hung them on the door to the back of the shop desperately trying to provide a little sound proofing, Jim reached for his mobile swiping at it frantically until it emitted music. Anthony at the till stepped forward, waved his hand around as best he could to attract Afonso’s attention, and once satisfied he grabbed it, Anthony looked Afonso straight in the eye, spread his arms wide and declared, “Welcome to Legal Jims ! What’ll you have ?”

Epilogue

Epilogue

SIX MONTHS LATER

In the midst of an intense conversation Kathryn turned to Jim and said, "Do you remember that meal at the Mexican ?" Jim nodded. "I said I was going to record data as to mental health hospital admissions, crime figures, house prices, the happiness index as of then, half a year ago, and so I could compare them against future data. Well I did it, and in the last couple of days I've collected the data as it now."

"And ?"

"Well it is incredible but there has been a marked reduction in the number of person being sectioned under the mental health act. Muggings have dropped off the chart,"

"Must be the love in the air ?" Suggested Jim.

"Burglaries are down as are thefts of all sort and domestic violence. House prices have risen for the third consecutive month and of the thirty-two London Boroughs Croydon now ranks number one on the happiness index. I can't believe it Jim but seriously genuinely absolutely everything has got better since your shop opened."

"Knew it would be." grinned Jim, and he reached out to Kathryn and she reached out to him and mutually they pulled each other close and simply lay there together stark bollock naked.

Printed in Great Britain
by Amazon

46149522R00103